D0828657

Meet the Mommies-To-Be...

Liz Van Zandt

My twin sis Bridget and I are so much alike—even our biological clocks are synchronized! As girls, we made a deal to start our families, regardless of our marital status, at age 30. Well, here we are at the big 3-0 and all I need is a fine male specimen to offer up his DNA. But how am I ever going to make my baby dreams come true when I keep finding myself lip-locked with the fabulously wealthy, utterly masculine Eric Statler?

Hey…

Bridget Van Zandt

My sister Liz may have entered this world four minutes before me, but this time I got the jump on *her*. While she's scrambling for a "suitable donor," I'm basking in full-fledged pregnancy. Who needs modern man when you've got modern science! Still, one gorgeous guy *has* blipped across my husband-radar—black sheep bachelor Nick Raines. And one lightning-bolt kiss from Nick and I'm suddenly wishing I'd waited to make my little darling the old-fashioned way!

Dear Reader,

Harlequin American Romance is celebrating the holidays with four wonderful books for you to treasure all season long, starting with the latest installment in the RETURN TO TYLER series. Bestselling author Judy Christenberry charms us with her delightful story of a sought-after bachelor who finds himself falling for a single mother and longing to become part of her *Patchwork Family*.

In Pamela Browning's *Baby Christmas*, soon after a department store Santa urges a lovely woman to make a wish on Christmas Eve, she finds a baby on her doorstep and meets a handsome handyman. To win custody of her nephew, a loving aunt decides her only resource is to pretend to be engaged to a *Daddy, M.D.* Don't miss this engaging story from Jacqueline Diamond.

Rounding out the month is Harlequin American Romance's innovative story, *Twin Expectations* by Kara Lennox. In this engaging volume, identical twin sisters pledge to become mothers—with or without husbands—by their thirtieth birthday. As the baby hunt heats up, the sisters unexpectedly find love with two gorgeous half brothers.

Next month, look for Harlequin American Romance's spin-off of TEXAS CONFIDENTIAL, Harlequin Intrigue's in-line continuity series, and another WHO'S THE DADDY? title from Muriel Jensen.

I hope you enjoy all our romance novels this month. All of us at Harlequin Books wish you a wonderful holiday season!

Melissa Jeglinski
Associate Senior Editor
Harlequin American Romance

TWIN EXPECTATIONS
Kara Lennox

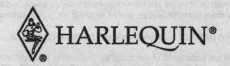

HARLEQUIN®

TORONTO • NEW YORK • LONDON
AMSTERDAM • PARIS • SYDNEY • HAMBURG
STOCKHOLM • ATHENS • TOKYO • MILAN • MADRID
PRAGUE • WARSAW • BUDAPEST • AUCKLAND

ISBN 0-373-16856-X

TWIN EXPECTATIONS

This edition published by arrangement with Harlequin Books S.A.

® and TM are trademarks of the publisher. Trademarks indicated with ® are registered in the United States Patent and Trademark Office, the Canadian Trade Marks Office and in other countries.

Visit us at www.eHarlequin.com

Printed in U.S.A.

ABOUT THE AUTHOR

Texas native Kara Lennox has been an art director, typesetter, advertising copy writer, textbook editor and reporter. She's worked in a boutique, a health club and has conducted telephone surveys. She's been an antiques dealer and briefly ran a clipping service. But no work has made her happier than writing romance novels.

When Kara isn't writing, she indulges in an ever-changing array of weird hobbies, from rock-climbing to crystal digging. But her mind is never far from her stories. Just about anything can send her running to her computer to jot down a new idea for some future novel.

Books by Kara Lennox

HARLEQUIN AMERICAN ROMANCE

Don't miss any of our special offers. Write to us at the following address for information on our newest releases.

Harlequin Reader Service
U.S.: 3010 Walden Ave., P.O. Box 1325, Buffalo, NY 14269
Canadian: P.O. Box 609, Fort Erie, Ont. L2A 5X3

THE OFFICIAL BIOLOGICAL CLOCK
PLEDGE

We, Bridget Van Zandt and Elizabeth Van Zandt,
being of sane, sound minds, want to someday
raise families. However, families usually require
husbands, which neither of us have—yet. Should
we reach the age of thirty and still be unmarried,
un-engaged and with no serious boyfriends, we
hereby solemnly swear, pledge, promise and affirm
that we will attempt to have babies anyway, using
whatever means we feel is appropriate.

Signed,

Bridget Van Zandt

Liz Van Zandt

Prologue

"So, do you feel any different?" Liz Van Zandt asked her twin sister, Bridget. They sat in the front seat of Liz's shiny new Miata in the parking lot of the Statler Clinic.

Bridget fidgeted with the hem of her denim skirt. "No. Do you think I should?"

"How should I know?" Liz said. "I've never been pregnant. But it probably hasn't happened yet. I've read that it can take hours, even days, for those little suckers to swim to the target."

Bridget felt light-headed. She placed a protective hand over her abdomen, knowing Liz was just trying to rattle her cage. Liz, older by four minutes, was all in favor of Bridget having a baby. She just didn't entirely approve of Bridget's methods.

"You're not having second thoughts, are you, Bridge?" Liz asked.

"It's a little late for those." No, she wasn't having second thoughts. She and Liz had always agreed that if they hit thirty and were unmarried, they would attempt motherhood anyway. Together. "Still, it'd be nice if there was a father in the picture."

Liz's eyes sparkled with mischief. "You might as well give up that notion. Men run from single moms as if they have leprosy."

"I don't care," Bridget said defiantly. "In twenty-one days, I'll come back to the Statler Clinic and find out whether I'm pregnant."

Liz sagged against the leather seat. "I guess it's my turn. I'd better get cracking."

"Oh, Liz, you aren't really going to carry through with your harebrained plan, are you?"

"It's not harebrained. I want to know exactly what kind of genetic material my baby is getting."

"You can't just tackle some man on the street and say, 'Hey, could you give me some of your DNA?'"

"I plan to be a little more subtle. If I can even find a suitable...donor..." Liz's eyes glazed over, and she stared at something in the distance. "Oo-la-la, there's one now."

Bridget gasped as she realized the subject of her sister's appraisal. "Is that who I think it is?"

"It's him, all right. He was on the cover of *Inside Texas* a couple of months ago. I recognize every blue-blood inch of him. And he's even more gorgeous in person."

The man in question, J. Eric Statler III, had just come waltzing out of the clinic that bore his name.

"What the heck is he doing here?" Liz asked.

"He does own the clinic," Bridget pointed out.

"He owns half of Oaksboro," Liz said, which was almost true. The Statler Clinic was only a tiny piece of the Statler empire, which included hospitals, oil companies, newspapers, restaurants and a tennis-shoe manufacturing plant. He had businesses scattered throughout north Texas. He even owned the ad agency where Liz worked.

Liz sighed. "He's rich and good-looking, but nice, too. In that magazine article, it says he donates a lot of money to several local charities."

"That doesn't mean he'll donate his DNA," Bridget said. "And if he's so perfect, then why hasn't he ever married?"

"Hasn't found the right woman, so I hear." Liz got a thoughtful look on her face. "Maybe he's waiting for me."

"Dream on, sister."

"Now, wait a minute. I'm a successful account executive at Oaksboro's biggest ad agency, I can eat fettuccini without making a mess, and I'm a darn nice person. Are you saying I wouldn't be a good match for Eric Statler?"

Uh-oh. Bridget recognized that gleam in Liz's eye.

"All right, maybe he wouldn't marry me," Liz continued, "but he's good father material."

"Liz, you don't even know him."

"I could meet him. It would be easy. I have contacts."

Bridget laughed. "You're nuts." But she could tell Liz was warming to this idea, another one of her crazy schemes.

Suddenly Liz focused her sea-blue eyes on Bridget with the force of double laser beams. "Hey, Bridge, will you help me?"

Bridget cringed. When Liz got that light of zeal in her eyes, nothing could stop her. "I have a few contacts I could tap, I suppose," she agreed reluctantly. She decided she'd better keep an eye on her competitive sister. If Bridget's artificial insemination worked and she ended up pregnant, Liz would be desperate to keep up. And no telling what she might do in her quest for, as she so elegantly put it, a "donor."

Chapter One

Bridget sipped her club soda nervously as she surveyed the jewel- and tux-bedecked crowd around her. Normally she favored a little something with the soda. But now that she was pregnant...

She paused in her thoughts, savoring the word. *Pregnant.* Today she'd had her official pregnancy test at the Statler Clinic. The results had only confirmed what she'd already known. At just three weeks from conception, her body was changing in some slight, indefinable way.

In a few months she would start expanding like a dashboard airbag. The prospect was scary but kind of exciting, too.

"See anyone we can mingle with?" asked Liz, standing beside her. They'd wangled invitations to the Oilman's Ball from a dry-cleaning baroness, a family friend whose portrait Bridget had painted. The ball was Oaksboro's social event of the season, and Eric Statler was guaranteed to be in attendance. But now that they'd arrived, the hard work began—finding someone who would provide Liz with a personal introduction to Statler.

"I've never been that great at mingling," Bridget replied. "Wait...over there. Are those Eric Statler's parents?" She nodded toward a distinguished-looking couple who appeared to be holding court.

"That's them, all right," Liz said. "Geraldine and Eric Statler, Jr. Everyone calls Mr. Statler 'Two,' you know. Because he didn't like 'Junior.'"

"And the son?" Bridget wanted to know. "Do they call him 'Three?'"

"They call him just plain Eric," Liz said, her eyes scanning the crowd.

"How do you know so much about the Statlers?"

"The Internet. Wait, I see one of our agency's clients," Liz said. "Let's split up. We can cover more territory that way."

Bridget nodded, only too happy to step away from Liz. They'd foolishly forgotten to check with each other beforehand, and they'd worn nearly identical dresses. Even their shoulder-length blond hair was styled in a similar fashion. That was one of the hazards of being a psychically attuned twin.

Liz winked at Bridget, then took off, leaving Bridget to find someone of her own to mingle with. Fortunately, she spotted Mrs. Hampton, the dry-cleaning baroness.

"Bridget, I'm so pleased you could make it," the stylish silver-haired matron said as Bridget approached. "There's a lovely couple I want you to meet. I bet they're in the market for a portrait."

Though she was booked through the summer, Bridget was always pleased at the prospect of new business. And, who could tell, maybe this couple knew Eric Statler.

She'd thought this romantic goal of Liz's was crazy at first. But the more she'd thought about it, the more she'd come to realize that Liz *would* make a good match for Statler. She had the social skills, the assertiveness, the self-confidence to keep up with someone who moved in his circles, whereas Bridget, while appreciating the man's finer qualities, knew she would prefer a…quieter marriage.

Mrs. Hampton trundled off, dragging Bridget gamely behind her.

NICHOLAS RAINES drained his second gin-and-tonic and stifled a yawn. He despised these functions, but his mother had laid a guilt trip on him about attending. It was for charity, she'd said. It was a chance to see and be seen, make important business contacts, blah-blah-blah. She'd even hinted that he might meet a woman, as if he had time for a relationship. Still, if a mother couldn't count on her own son to buy a ticket to a charity ball when she was on the committee, who could she count on?

He hoped the charity—a women's shelter—raked in a bundle. But he'd yet to meet anyone this evening with whom he had the slightest interest in doing business. As for running into an appealing woman, what a joke. Practically every woman here was either over sixty, married or both.

He wondered how long he had to stay. Till the auction, he supposed. If he didn't bid on something, he'd never hear the end of it from his mother. He was already in trouble because he hadn't worn a tux. Maybe he could hide behind one of those big potted trees until the—

His thoughts froze. *Who* was *that?* She was under sixty, that was for sure. Maybe even under thirty. She wasn't wearing a wedding ring, he noticed right away. And he'd never laid eyes on her before, because he would have remembered that face. So she wasn't a regular among this crowd. They had that in common to start with.

He grabbed two glasses of champagne from a passing waiter and approached the woman, noting with pleasure that she got even prettier the closer he came. She looked up, smiling boldly as he held out his offering to her.

"Oh, champagne!" she said, her blue eyes sparkling with enthusiasm. "Thank you. I'm Liz Van Zandt. And who might you..." Her voice trailed off, and her gaze focused on something faraway and over his left shoulder. He turned to look, then felt a momentary deflation when he saw what had snagged her attention.

Eric. Why did his handsome, rich, and well-meaning little brother always intrude at the wrong time? Social situations, business, it didn't matter. Didn't he know how annoying perfection could be?

"Is something wrong, Miss Van Zandt?" Now, what the hell was her first name? Faces stayed in his brain on permanent record, but he had an appalling memory when it came to names.

"Huh? Oh, sorry." The woman returned her attention to Nick. "I believe that's Eric Statler, near the podium," she said casually.

"Yeah. That's Eric, all right."

"You know him?" she asked hopefully.

"Yeah."

"Really?" She continued to study Eric with un-disguised hunger. "Is he as smart and hardworking as everyone says?"

"He's an okay guy," Nick was forced to admit. It would be so much easier if he could hate Eric, but he couldn't. His younger, half brother was pretty cool.

The woman continued to wax enthusiastic. "I was just doing some reading about Eric Statler. This one article said he baled his black-sheep brother's airline out of bankruptcy, took it over, then fired him. Or the brother quit, no one's sure."

"The brother quit," Nick confirmed, gritting his teeth. That wretched magazine story, back to haunt him again. Eric had bought up a majority share in Lone Star Air so that his half brother would be free to fund a new start-up. That was what Nick did best. Lone Star wasn't, and never had been, near bank-ruptcy, but the press loved to twist things around, give commonplace events more drama.

"Oh, so then you must know the real story," she said. "Not that I'm into gossip, but I had a feeling the magazine account wasn't accurate. Care to en-lighten me?"

"Why are you interested?" Nick wanted to know.

"Because I want to discuss business with him. And I'd like to have the facts before I do."

Nick shook his head. He'd already spent far too much of his life apologizing for his position within the Statler family. He'd vowed not to do it again. He was over that, on to bigger and better things.

"The matter's confidential," he said.

"Hmm. Well, in that case, is there any chance you could introduce me to him?"

Maybe that wasn't such a bad idea, Nick conceded. This woman was gorgeous, but in the last thirty seconds he'd decided she wasn't his type. Too brassy, too forward. And she was spreading lies about him, to boot, although not intentionally.

"I might be able to arrange an introduction." Yeah, he'd like to watch his brother handle this hot potato. Women came at Eric by the dozens, with strategies both subtle and obvious. He was curious to see what this one would try.

He held out his arm. "Come with me, Ms. Van Zandt. I'll take you to meet my brother."

"Who?"

"My brother. Eric Statler. You told me your name, but I neglected to tell you mine. It's Nick Raines."

He enjoyed the look of discomfiture on the pretty blonde's face. He could read her thoughts. She was torn. Should she apologize for that "black-sheep" business? Or should she recover her dignity as best she could and make her escape?

LIZ WISHED she could sink right into the carpet. She'd stumbled into a golden opportunity—meeting Eric Statler's half brother—and she'd bungled it. Foot-in-mouth disease was one of her shortcomings. She was bubbly, talkative, not at all shy like Bridget, and she was tops on the invitation list to just about any party, but she had a distinct problem when it came to tact. Sometimes words just came out of her mouth, by-passing her brain entirely.

"I apologize for any hurtful remarks," she finally

said when she'd recovered her composure. "I hadn't realized who you were, of course, or I might have been more discreet."

"Don't worry, I've been insulted by worse than you," Nick Raines said easily. "Invitation's still good. Want to meet Eric?"

Liz swallowed her embarrassment. "Sure, I'd like that." She took Nick's proffered arm and allowed him to lead her through the crowd. He was a nice-looking man, she conceded, but not her type at all. He had a solemnity to his personality, a shadow in his eyes, that wouldn't mix well with her fun-loving attitude. She could see him more easily dating someone like Bridget, who could spend hours just reading poetry or studying the play of light and shadow in a tree.

Maybe, once she made friends with Eric, she would get Nick and Bridget together. But right now, she had to focus on her own impending moment of truth. Nick was leading her unerringly toward her target, Oaksboro's golden boy himself.

Even from several feet away she could feel his charisma. He was undeniably handsome, yes, with his blond, suntanned, clean-cut good looks. Piercing blue eyes, square jaw, broad shoulders, commanding height—clearly no one could argue his physical appeal. But it was more than that. He carried himself with a certain arrogance, yet his smile was friendly, and she could tell that he listened attentively whenever anyone spoke to him.

Her heart beat double time. What was she going to say to him? She'd better have one hell of an opening line or she wouldn't stand a chance, not when so many of his admirers were attractive female types.

Eric looked up as Nick and Liz approached. "There you are," he said to Nick. "Mother's been looking for you."

"Terrific." Nick pulled Eric aside to where they could converse semiprivately. "Eric, I'd like you to meet Ms. Van Zandt."

Liz held out her hand, still trying to come up with that perfect *bon mot* that would catch and hold this magnificent man's attention. "It's Liz," she said smoothly. And then the words just poured out of her mouth. "My sister is very grateful to you."

"And why is that?" Eric asked pleasantly, shaking her hand. His hand was strong, his grip firm. He listened to her with that same undivided attention she'd seen him devote to others, and it unnerved her.

"Well, she's pregnant, and in a way you're responsible!"

Eric's smile froze. "Ms. Van Zandt, I don't take accusations of that nature lightly—"

"Oh, wait, that came out all wrong—"

"One more word, and you'll be talking to my lawyers, is that clear?"

"I didn't mean it the way it sounded—"

"This conversation is over. I don't wish to make a scene at a charity event, but I trust I won't lay eyes on you again this evening." He turned and strode away.

Liz turned toward Nick, so she could at least explain to *him* what she'd meant, but the crowd had claimed him, also.

"Foot-in-mouth disease strikes again," Liz murmured. She skulked away, wondering how she was going to explain her utter, humiliating failure to Bridget.

"TEHRE YOU ARE," Mrs. Hampton said, limping arthritically toward Bridget, who was doing her best imitation of wallpaper. Again. She just wasn't any good at parties. "My, such a crowd here. You are having a good time, aren't you?"

"Well, not as good as Liz," Bridget couldn't resist remarking. Her sister really knew how to work a party. She mingled, she chitchatted, she glowed.

"Oh, you know how Liz is," Mrs. Hampton said, patting Bridget's hand as she pulled her along. "Come, now, there's someone else I want you to meet. This one is in the art supply business. Now, promise me you won't talk shop all night."

"Promise," Bridget said. Lord, could this get any worse? She wished brazen Liz would just walk right up to Eric Statler and introduce herself. Then Bridget could consider the night a success and go home.

"Here we are. Bridget Van Zandt, meet Fred Santoro."

"How do you do, Mr.—"

The pudgy, fiftyish man shook her hand while his gaze focused firmly on her cleavage. "Nice to meet you, honey. Say, that's some dress. Really displays the goods to perfection, know what I mean?"

Yikes! She was afraid she did. She looked helplessly for Mrs. Hampton, who had immediately disappeared.

"You married, little lady?"

Oh, barfola. *Little lady?* "Um, well—"

He upped the wattage of his leer. "Ah, I see. No ring. You must be one of these liberated gals, don't want to be tied down with a kitchen and kids. Yeah, I understand." He winked, then took her arm and tried to lead her away. At such close proximity, she could smell overindulgence on his breath. "Do you like Cadillacs?"

Bridget dug in her heels. "Let me go."

"What's the matter, honey?" he asked, genuinely befuddled. Maybe this approach usually worked for him, but she couldn't imagine how.

"Listen, Mr. Santoro, I'm not your honey and I'm not going anywhere with you."

He looked skeptical.

Feeling panicked, she resorted to a lie. "There's my husband, that's him, right over there." She pointed to a complete stranger who stood out from the crowd, and not just because of his clothing. He was tall. And gorgeous. And a bit out of place in this fancy gilt ballroom with his outdoorsy good looks. She could picture him riding a horse or chopping wood or paddling a kayak.

He watched her, amused for some reason.

Her mouth went dry. My, my, why hadn't Mrs. Hampton introduced her to *him?*

Mr. Santoro immediately released her. "Oh, um, sorry, there, now, didn't mean to step on any toes." He literally backed away, ducking his head, holding his hands out as if beseeching forgiveness before disappearing behind an ice sculpture.

"I see you've made another conquest."

Bridget nearly jumped out of her high heels. The man—the fictitious husband—had materialized at her side, and he was looking at her through intriguing gray eyes with a mixture of amusement and disapproval. Surely he hadn't been standing close enough a few moments ago to hear her fib to Mr. Santoro.

"I, um, apologize for pointing at you," she said, stumbling on every word. "But that man was…I told him you were my, er, husband just to get rid of him. I hope I didn't embarrass you."

He shrugged. "As long as you don't hold me to it."

She looked at him quizzically. "Well, of course not."

"Did you have a nice chat with my brother? Sorry I didn't stick around after the introductions."

"Who?" Bridget asked, even more confused. And then it hit her. This man, this gorgeous man with the steely eyes and the rebellious wardrobe, thought she was Liz. Her social-butterfly sister must have already gotten to him. And, Bridget thought, judging from the way he'd been sparring with her, Liz had probably done something to provoke him.

She was about to explain about her twin when he asked, "Exactly how many glasses of champagne have you had?"

She drew herself up. "None. I can't drink alcohol because I'm…well, I'm pregnant." There, she'd admitted it. She wasn't planning to keep it a secret, after all, and in another three months or so she wouldn't be able to, anyway.

His teasing smile fell away. "Congratulations. I guess that means I'll have to stop flirting with you. If I don't want your husband to deck me, that is."

"You don't have to worry about that," she said as matter-of-factly as she dared. "I'm not married."

"Well, the baby's father, then," he said, frowning.

"I wouldn't even know who that is. You see, I was art—"

"No need for explanations." The look he gave her was suddenly cold, uncompromising. And definitely disapproving.

"But it's not what you think. You see—"

He actually backed away from her. "Really. Enough said."

"Will you let me finish?"

He waited for her to go on, but his expression was so implacable she suddenly couldn't imagine what possessed her to confide anything to him.

"Oh, never mind," she finally said in a much cooler tone. "I guess this isn't the time or place to defend a lifestyle choice. But I might caution you not to make snap judgments. 'Enough said' is a convenient way of cutting off what you *think* you don't want to hear." She turned away, tears burning at the back of her eyes.

"Wait. You never told me what you thought of my brother."

Bridget, longing to flee this train wreck of a conversation, paused. A sneaking suspicion occurred to her.

"Your brother...?"

"Eric," he supplied, a tad impatiently.

Bridget just nodded. If she tried to explain now about Liz, things would only get more confusing. "Nice guy," she said, then made good her escape.

NICE GUY?

Nick watched her retreat with mixed feeling. Earlier he'd decided she wasn't his type, only to reconsider a few moments ago. Just now she'd seemed funny and vulnerable and altogether his type, and he'd been questioning his sanity in dismissing her before. He'd been crazy to introduce her to Eric! Then she'd blithely announced she was pregnant, sans husband, and he'd had to revise his opinion yet again.

Her announcement had truly surprised him. Didn't anybody get married and have families in a normal way these days? He didn't like to think of himself as a judgmental kind of person, but he supposed he was. Not about everything. But the irresponsible conception of children hit a nerve. His unmarried mother hadn't meant to get pregnant with him, but she had. And he'd endured the consequences, both before and after her marriage to his stepfather, Eric Statler, Jr.

If Ms. Van Zandt—he still couldn't remember her first name—was so careless about bringing another life into the world, that was her choice. Still, part of him wished he hadn't alienated her. Even now he felt a tremendous urge to scour the ballroom until he found her again and apologize—for what, he didn't know.

SO, BRIDGET THOUGHT when she was safely away from the self-superior lout, she'd been talking to Eric Statler's brother and hadn't even realized it. Apparently Liz hadn't been as slow-witted. She'd finagled an introduction to Eric.

Good for her! Mission accomplished. Now all

Bridget wanted was to get out of this stuffy ballroom and kick off her heels. First, however, she had to locate Liz and find out how the meeting went.

She looked all over but couldn't find her twin. How was it that a woman as flamboyant and noticeable as Liz could manage to become invisible?

She checked the ladies' room. No Liz. Nor could she be found at the bar, or at the long tables where items for the upcoming auction were displayed.

She trolled the ballroom one more time and suddenly found herself only a few feet from Eric Statler himself. She'd never been this close to him, and she found herself stopping and staring. He was quite a magnificent specimen of man, but not nearly as intriguing as his brother. Bridget found herself comparing the two men. Eric was handsome, but his face wasn't as mature looking as Nicholas's. There was more of a boyish quality there, though his eyes had a certain determined set to them. Yes, that combination would appeal to Liz.

The crowd shifted, and Bridget stood mere inches away from the millionaire philanthropist.

Suddenly Eric turned. He made eye contact with Bridget. Immediately his smile froze, his face reddened, and he darn near snarled.

"I thought I told you not to come near me again."

Chapter Two

Bridget's mind worked furiously. What on earth had Liz done? "I think there must be some—"

"Save your breath, Ms. Van Zandt. I don't listen to money-grubbing little gold diggers. If you'd like to pursue a paternity suit, go ahead. But you'd better know you won't win. I won't pay off your sister just to get rid of the annoyance, and a DNA test will prove unequivocally that I am not the father of her baby."

As the great man spoke, he motioned to someone with his hand. In seconds, two security guards had Bridget by the elbows.

"Escort Ms. Van Zandt out of the ballroom, please," Eric instructed the guards. "And see that she doesn't get back in."

Bridget looked around with the faint hope that someone would rescue her. Mrs. Hampton, maybe? But she saw nothing but the faces of strangers, some hostile, some amused.

The guards led her away. The crowd parted. People stared. This was the worst moment of Bridget's life, and she was going to kill Liz when she saw her again.

NICK FELT a strange sense of loss as the security guards led the pretty blond woman away. He had to know what was going on. Normally his staid, oh-so-respectable brother did not make scenes.

"What was that all about?" he asked as soon as he could get his half brother's attention.

Eric rolled his eyes. "Man, has she got some nerve. She thinks she'll make a fast buck by naming me as the father of a baby I had nothing to do with. She obviously doesn't know me very well."

Despite the brave talk, Eric looked a bit shaken, and Nick couldn't blame him. Eric had been wary of women ever since a casual girlfriend in college had tried to decimate both his reputation and his bank account by pulling a similar stunt.

Nick wasn't quite sure how to phrase his next question. As an older brother, he'd often cautioned Eric about the wily ways of women and how to avoid the worst of the pitfalls. But he hadn't had such a brotherly conversation in, oh, ten years. Still, he blundered forward.

"Um, Eric, you don't know that woman, do you?"

"You mean *know?* As in the Biblical sense?" Eric laughed. "I never laid eyes on her till about ten minutes ago. Are you having a good time?" he asked, moving away from the knot of people he'd been conversing with so the brothers could have a rare, private conversation. "I'm surprised you're here at all. You've always hated these things." He gave a disapproving once-over to Nick's attire, but said nothing about it.

"Mom did a number on me," Nick admitted without any real venom.

"She brought up that Steuben vase again?"

Nick nodded. When he'd shattered the vase with a badly aimed Frisbee twenty-five years ago, he'd never dreamed the incident would stay with him this long.

"With me it's the crumpled fender on her Lincoln," Eric said ruefully. "Gets me every time. You staying for the auction?"

"Yeah. I promised I'd buy something, though I can't imagine there's anything here I really need."

Eric flashed a wicked grin. "I know the perfect thing, and you'll make Mother ecstatic. You know how she's been after you for years to get your portrait done?"

"Yeah…" Nick said cautiously. He'd been on the hot seat about this portrait thing ever since Eric had caved in and had his done—seated in the library, no less, looking a lot like his grandfather had in his prime.

"A local artist donated an oil portrait. She's supposed to be good. Bid on that. Kill two birds with one stone."

Sure, why not? Nick thought. It was for charity, after all.

He and Eric caught up on a few business details having to do with the airline, then Nick wandered off. He thought about leaving the ballroom to check on the Van Zandt woman, then realized how misplaced his concern was. If she was ballsy enough to threaten Eric Statler with a paternity suit, she could take care of herself. And she certainly wasn't anyone he needed to know better.

BRIDGET SAT DOWNSTAIRS in the hotel lobby, her eyes trained on the elevators. Liz would have to come down sooner or later, and when she did, Bridget intended to take a strip off her sister's hide. Not only would Liz never get a date with Eric Statler, no decent man would come near either of them because they'd be fearful of getting slapped with a paternity suit.

What on earth had Liz said to Eric? Or to Nick, for that matter? They couldn't have engineered a worse fiasco if they'd tried. No wonder they hadn't found husbands.

Bridget recognized several of the formally dressed people who exited the elevators. She kept her head ducked, praying they wouldn't recognize her. She only hoped she didn't have to move away from Oaksboro after this misadventure. Although the city had grown tremendously and was getting more cosmopolitan every day, it was still a small town. That small-town gossip grapevine was certainly alive and well.

At last Liz appeared, looking worried. "There you are!" she exclaimed, striding over to where Bridget was seated. "I've been looking all over for you. What are you doing down here?"

"I was kicked out of the ball," Bridget said succinctly, glowering at her sister. "Because of something *you* said to Eric Statler."

Liz gasped. "Oh, no!"

"Oh, yes. Mrs. Hampton will be scandalized. Mother will go into hiding. What on earth did you say to the man?"

Liz flopped down defeatedly on the sofa across from Bridget. "It was supposed to be funny. You know, just a witticism to get his attention."

"What…did…you…say?"

"Well, I said something about how grateful you were to him because you were pregnant. You know, because he owns the clinic and all…"

"Oh, Liz! How could you?"

"I had to say something to catch his attention. You saw how swamped he was with people wanting to talk to him."

"Never mind. I don't want to hear any more."

Liz continued relentlessly. "Once I had his attention I was going to explain, and, well, my witticism was about as funny as a nuclear bomb."

"Yeah, no kidding."

"How was I to know the man is so sensitive?" She sighed when Bridget didn't respond. "Wanting Eric Statler to father my child was the stupidest idea I've ever had."

"Amen. Let's just get out of here. Then we can proceed with the business of moving to Las Vegas and changing our names."

"Aw, come on, Sis, it's not that bad," Liz said as she walked Bridget to her car. "I mean, if you look at it in a certain way, it's funny. You should have seen Statler's face. It turned the most interesting shade of—"

"It's not funny. It'll never be funny," Bridget snapped. She paused as she stuck the key into her car door, overcome by a sudden light-headedness. She steadied herself by grabbing Liz's arm, then took a deep breath. The moment passed.

"Bridge, are you okay?"

Liz's sudden and very real concern did a lot toward erasing Bridget's anger. It was hard to stay mad at Liz, who always meant well.

"Just a little dizzy moment," she said. "Dr. Keller said not to be surprised if I felt light-headed from time to time."

Pregnant. She was pregnant, and the baby would be born some time around the end of February.

She started to turn the key in the lock when she heard a noise beside her. It was Liz, and she was crying.

"Liz?"

"I w-want to have a dizzy spell," she said. "I want to be pregnant, too. Now that I've blown it with Eric, I'll have to start all over finding a donor."

Bridget put her arm around her twin's shoulders. "It'll happen, Liz. You've got plenty of time to find the right, um, donor."

"But we've always done everything together."

Bridget realized she'd done her share of fantasizing about her and Liz waddling down the street together, both of them big as houses. Pushing matching strollers to the park. Trading baby clothes.

"I'm just being silly," Liz finally said. "Being an aunt is cool, too." She enveloped Bridget in a bear hug, and they both cried.

SIX WEEKS LATER, at about 7:00 a.m., Bridget envied her unpregnant sister. She lay in bed, her eyes closed and reached blindly for the saltines on the nightstand. This was her mother's surefire cure for morning sickness—nibble a few saltines before opening your eyes.

After making sure her bed was good and full of crumbs, Bridget opened one eye experimentally. So far, so good. She opened the other eye. No nausea.

This was amazing! She really did feel okay. She sat up slowly, then stood and put on her robe. Maybe she could even eat some cereal. She padded to the kitchen to put the kettle on for tea. September sun streamed cheerfully in through the window.

Bridget opened the back door to get a little breeze. She inhaled deeply taking in the fresh morning air, then got a whiff of whatever her neighbors were cooking for breakfast. Bacon, she realized just as her stomach revolted. She made a mad dash for the bathroom, barely making it.

Great. In a short time she had an appointment with the man who'd bought her portrait donation from the Oilman's Ball charity auction. He'd paid an unheard of fifty-two hundred dollars for the painting. Bridget's usual price would have been something closer to half that amount.

She'd already rescheduled the appointment once. Since the man had paid so much, she didn't feel right about canceling again. She would just have to get through it somehow.

Her stomach settled as she headed for the address she'd been given, a few miles south of town. Once she had her bearings, she gave some thought to the portrait she was to paint. Usually her subjects had an idea of what they wanted, but if this man didn't, she had to be prepared with some suggestions. It would help if she knew what he looked like, or at least what age he was.

His name was Quinn, or something like that. She'd received only a card with the name scribbled in barely legible writing, and a phone number to contact. She'd never even spoken to him—only to his secretary.

She made several false turns before she located the correct address, and then she wondered if she'd misread it. She found herself in a cluster of ramshackle buildings sorely in need of paint. A faded sign announced that this was "Peachy's Air Freight Co." The slogan underneath assured wary customers, "We fly anything, anywhere."

The nose of one rickety airplane, a World War II relic, was visible in a falling-down hangar.

Egad, how could someone who worked here—or even someone who owned the place—afford over five thousand dollars for a portrait?

She pulled in front of the most prominent building, hoping it was the main entrance, and got out of her car. Her low-heeled pumps crunched against sand and gravel as she made her way to the door.

The office was a nightmare of shag carpeting and stale cigarette stench, calendar landscapes hung crookedly in plastic frames, and a fake plant so encrusted with dust it was gray instead of green.

The young woman at the front desk, however, appeared pleasant. She offered a smile. "Are you the artist?"

Bridget smiled back and handed the receptionist a card. "Yes. Bridget Van Zandt."

"Then you'll be looking for my boss. He's out

working on the plane. I'd take you out there, but he'd kill me if I left the phone unmanned.''

"I'll find him," Bridget said, anxious to escape the stale cigarette smell before it set her stomach off. "I saw where the hangar is." She started to leave.

"Don't let him scare you," the receptionist offered. "He's not crazy about this portrait thing, but he'll go through with it if you pester him enough."

"Uh-huh. Thanks for the advice." Bridget successfully escaped the office this time, thinking there was no way she would "pester" Mr. Quinn. If he didn't want his portrait painted, that was fine with her. She had plenty of other work to get done. Not that she minded doing a charity painting now and then, but now that she had the baby to think about, she took her income a little more seriously.

She rounded the corner into the hangar and stopped. There before her was the most gorgeous set of male buns she'd ever seen. They were encased in snug, faded denim. The man they were attached to stood on a ladder, his head and shoulders buried in the engine of the beat-up twin-engine plane.

"Mr. Quinn?" she called out once she caught her breath. Maybe she would change her mind about pestering him. Painting this man—his body, anyway—would be a pleasure.

"Be with you in a minute," he called back to her. His deep voice sounded distracted—and familiar. Where had she heard it, and why did it send a pleasurable shiver down her spine?

Her memory snapped the lost piece into place just about the time he pulled out of the airplane and looked down at her.

Oh, God, not him. But it was. Nick Raines, who looked every bit as rugged and dashing as he had the night of the Oilman's Ball, despite the smudge of grease on his face and the two days' growth of beard shadowing his cheek.

"I'm looking for Mr. Quinn," she said, trying to brazen it out. Maybe he wouldn't remember her.

"You're that woman from the charity thing," he said, his expression a mixture of fascination and horror. "The one who tried to rip off my brother."

"I did no such—" Bridget stopped herself as a wave of nausea washed over her. She would not get angry. Surely such a strongly negative emotion wouldn't be good for the baby. "I'm looking for a Mr. Quinn," she said primly, then peered at him hopefully through her lashes.

"There's no Mr. Quinn here." Nick came down from the ladder. "Don't tell me...you're the portrait artist?"

"Yes. It says right here on this card the auction people sent, M. Quinn." She yanked the card from her purse and stared hard at it. Raines. If she squinted her eyes just right, the badly formed letters shaped themselves into "N. Raines."

"Then there must be a mistake," he said brusquely, rummaging through a tool box. The tools, unlike everything else at Peachy Air Freight, were shiny and well cared for.

"I'm afraid the mistake was mine," she said miserably, then asked him point-blank, "Did you buy an oil portrait at that auction?"

"Yeah, but..." He looked up, seeming to really

see her for the first time. "You're the artist, you said? You're Moving Pictures, Inc.?"

"Yes. And I understand completely if you'd like to forget the whole thing, given the rather unusual circumstances. Please believe me, I had no idea it was you who bought the portrait. I misread the name."

"I'd like nothing better than to forget it," he said, pulling a rag from his back pocket and scrubbing his face, removing the oil mark. "But there's the matter of five thousand and something dollars—"

"Maybe you could sell it to someone else," she suggested rather desperately.

"Now who in their right mind is going to pay that kind of money for a picture?"

She couldn't help but take offense. "You did."

"And I've been regretting it ever since. Anyway, no one ever accused me of being in my right mind. You're probably thinking no one in their right mind would buy this dump. Right?"

Bridget had no reply to that, but she couldn't help but wonder how the former CEO of Lone Star Airlines had landed here. Liz had told her something about Eric Statler bailing his half brother out of trouble with the airline, then squeezing him out of power.

"Peachy's looks better on paper," he said, probably seeing the skepticism on her face. "Cash flow's not so hot, but Old Man Peachy put his profits into planes—old ones that he always intended to fix and never did. Some of them have been sitting in hangars for twenty-five years, waiting for me to come along and restore them to their former glory." He patted the shiny silver nose cone of his current project.

Bridget could only stare at Nick. He was certainly passionate about his business, and he almost glowed with that passion—the way other men glowed when talking about a sexual conquest. She was fascinated. And not a little hot and bothered.

That was how she wanted to paint him. And she did want to paint him, she realized. If only they could smooth over the circumstances of their first meeting. Maybe if she explained about Liz and her warped sense of humor.

"Why am I telling you this?" he asked abruptly.

"I don't know. Look, Mr. Raines, this is an awkward situation, but we can make the best of it. You paid for the portrait, and I made a commitment to deliver it. I would like to keep that commitment."

"Can you paint?" he asked, crossing his arms and leaning against a timber that supported the hangar.

Bridget looked up nervously, afraid the timber would give way and the roof would crash down on them. "I brought my portfolio with me if you'd like to—"

"Nah." He sighed. "I guess there's nothing to do but go ahead with it. What do you do, snap some instant pictures or something? I can get cleaned up."

Bridget was horrified at the thought. "I don't work from photographs," she said, "except as a supplement. Paintings done that way often turn out flat, and the people don't look right because a camera catches a single moment that may or may not reflect the subject's true essence."

"True essence, huh?" He took a couple of steps closer, until he invaded her personal space. "You think I have a true essence?"

Bridget tried to swallow, her mouth suddenly dry. Yes, he had an essence, all right, one that was all male. Standing this close, she could even catch a tantalizing hint of his scent, a combination of starch, soap and hard work. Everything in her that was female responded, reminding her just exactly what she'd been missing of late.

Still, she stood her ground. "I paint with a live subject. A quality oil portrait requires a commitment of a great deal of time and energy from both artist and model." She usually developed a unique intimacy with every subject she painted, too, but she decided not to elaborate to that degree with Nick Raines.

"Look, ma'am—"

"Bridget." He'd obviously forgotten her name, though his had been branded into her memory. Someday when she was senile, his name would be the only thing she remembered. "Bridget Van Zandt."

"Look, Bridget, I really don't have hours to spend posing for this picture. Isn't there any other way?"

"No." On this she wouldn't compromise. Her soul went into every painting she did. She had to do each portrait the best she knew how—especially one that might end up having high visibility. If she did a second-rate job on it, the negative publicity could ruin her business.

"Hell. My mother already has a space cleared on her wall for this thing. Guess we'll have to do it your way."

"It won't be that bad," she said, more eager than she ought to be. Hadn't she, a few minutes ago, been hoping "Mr. Quinn" would elect not to do the portrait after all? "A couple of hours here and there. My schedule is flexible. We'll work around yours."

He nodded. "Okay." The hard lines of his face softened. "You're being very reasonable about this, after what my brother did to you. You, um, aren't actually planning to sue him, are you?"

Anger rose up again. She consciously tamped it down and took two slow, deep breaths. "No, I'm not planning to sue anybody. The incident at the Oilman's Ball was an unfortunate misunderstanding involving my identical twin sister. Please, can we forget about it?"

He actually chuckled, but he didn't agree to drop the subject forever. Then he sobered. "Um, by the way, how is the baby? You're looking a little pale."

"Am I?" She wasn't surprised. She'd had a terrible shock to her system. And having him speak so casually about a baby she'd scarcely mentioned to *anyone...*

"You are pregnant, right? I mean, you didn't make that part up too?"

Chapter Three

"Yes, I'm pregnant, and can we just drop it, please?" Bridget said.

Judging from the warning flash in her eyes, Nick decided he'd better leave well enough alone. "Understood," he finally said. "So, how do we proceed?"

She relaxed a bit. "I'll leave my portfolio in your office. Go through it at your leisure. Pick out the portraits you're drawn to, the ones you really like. Be thinking of how you'd like to be portrayed—how you'd like to be remembered for posterity. I'll call back in a few days and we'll meet again, to mull over ideas. Is that satisfactory?"

"Yes, that meets with my approval," he said, matching her ultraprofessional, formal tone. Two could play at this game. Even as he tried to one-up her, he found himself fascinated with her, with the way she stood up for herself without being rude. He'd thought her too forward and brassy when he'd first met her, but in this case first impressions were wrong. She didn't come off that way now.

"You'll hear from me." She turned and walked

away with a clipped, no-nonsense gate. He watched her, focusing on the sway of her slim hips. How would she look in a few months, when her pregnancy advanced? Would she waddle?

Oddly, he found the mental picture pleasing when it shouldn't have been. Since when did the thought of a pregnant woman get him excited?

With a shrug he returned his attention to the engine of the old Dehavilland Comet he'd been working on when Bridget had appeared. Bridget. How had he ever forgotten such a cute name? It wouldn't slip his mind again.

A lot of other things slipped, though. Like his wrench. Suddenly he had fifty fingers, all of them coated with butter. He found himself looking up things in his repair manual that he should have known by heart. That infernal woman had ruined his concentration.

After an hour he gave up and went back to the office to check up on Dinah, his new receptionist. She was punctual, pleasant and a hard worker, but she lacked something in the initiative department. If he didn't specifically tell her to do it, it didn't get done.

"Is everything all right?" he asked.

"Sure. Phone doesn't ring much."

That was because most of Peachy's customers retired along with him.

"Oh, Mr. Raines? I don't want to be a bother, but my chair is broken." She pointed to a stack of kindling in the corner. "I've been using this stool, but my back—"

"Good heavens, Dinah, order yourself a new office

chair. A nice one.'' Nick took a good look around the office and winced. This was what Bridget Van Zandt had seen. This was her first impression of his business. "While you're at it, order yourself a new desk and a couple of customer chairs. Then call a carpet place. And a painter.'' He sniffed the air. "And a No Smoking sign.''

Dinah's eyes lit up like Christmas morning. "Really?''

"Really. I'll sign the purchase orders. Do it up nice.''

"Yes, sir! Oh, Mr. Raines, did you see these pictures?'' She pointed to an open photo album on her desk. He recognized it as Bridget's portfolio. "They're beautiful. I can't wait to see what she does with you.''

That statement planted all sorts of images in Nick's fertile mind, none of them involving oil paints and canvas. "Let me see.'' He leaned on a corner of Dinah's desk and flipped through the album. It took only three or four flips for him to admit that he was impressed. The portraits were beautiful—so realistic the models could almost walk off the page. These people breathed with energy and personality. He almost felt as if he knew them, just by studying their portraits.

He recognized the subject in one of the paintings, a local matron named Velma Hampton. The woman was not classically attractive, yet Bridget had managed to catch that spark of humor and openness that shone from within.

"I like this one, don't you?'' Dinah said, pointing to a cowboy. He stood by a worn wooden fence, holding a coil of rope and gazing out at a field dotted with cattle. "I think you should do yours outside. Maybe with one of your planes."

"Now that is an excellent idea." If he had to spend hour upon hour posing for this asinine portrait, at least he could do it outside, in comfortable clothes. And when it was done, his portrait would stand out among the coat-and-tie Statler men hanging in his mother's library. "Call the Van Zandt woman and tell her I've decided what I want. Make arrangements for her to meet me at dawn at my house—you remember how to get there, right?"

"Yes, but why don't you call her yourself?"

"That's what I hired you for," he quipped.

The fact of the matter was, Bridget unsettled him. He would undoubtedly be spending a good deal of time with her, and he intended to keep their relationship cool and professional. He was sure that was how she wanted it, too.

DAWN. *Dawn!* What had Bridget been thinking to blithely agree to such insanity? She couldn't possibly be presentable by 7:00 a.m., not if she had to stick her head in the toilet every five minutes. Unfortunately she didn't have Nick's home phone number, so she couldn't call and cancel. She would just have to pull herself together or stand him up, one of the two.

Dripping from her shower, she glared at herself in the mirror. Her eyes were puffy and her skin was pale. Makeup helped, but not much. She threw on the first clothes she could find, a pair of faded jeans and a white ribbed shirt.

Then she remembered that Liz had said the shirt made her breasts look bigger. Forget that. She didn't want Nick to think she was advertising. Initially she'd been intrigued by him—and still thought he was gorgeous—but since the Oilman's Ball she'd put any thoughts about getting to know him better right out of her mind.

She chose a red cotton blouse and a studded denim vest instead. By the time she'd dried her hair she felt almost presentable, though certainly far from her best. She tied her hair back with a red ribbon.

What did it matter, anyway? she grumbled as she gathered her sketch pad and pencils, a Polaroid camera, some light-reflecting boards, and an industrial-size bottle of Tums. He didn't have to look at her while she was painting him. And since he was the one who had specified this uncivilized hour, he could suffer the consequences.

Over the past few weeks Bridget had scoped out all of Oaksboro for every gas station and convenience store with a decent bathroom. She plotted her route to Nick's house so that several of these nausea-friendly pit stops were on the way. She stopped three times and still was only ten minutes late when she pulled into the driveway.

His house was beautiful, she noted with some surprise. She'd been expecting to see something in the same state of disrepair as his business. But this charming, white frame house looked as if every square inch was lovingly cared for, right down to the marigolds and zinnias in the front flower beds.

That was all the time she had to study Nick's domicile. He burst out the front door as soon as her car pulled up, and all her attention became focused on him.

"You're late," he said in lieu of a greeting as she got out of the car. He seemed more anxious than irritated, though.

"I apologize," she said in a carefully neutral tone, mindful of the negative impact anger could have on her body chemistry. She offered no explanation for her tardiness. For some reason the thought of Nick knowing she'd succumbed to something as weak and...*female* as morning sickness filled her with apprehension.

She started toward her trunk, where her supplies were stored, but he grabbed her arm. "No time for that. I want you to see something before the light is ruined. Come on."

He more or less dragged her along the red brick path that went around the house. The path was uneven, making her glad she'd decided against hose and heels this morning. She was having enough trouble in her sneakers.

From the backyard they climbed over a wooden fence. That's when Bridget saw what he wanted her to see. Parked in the middle of a field was a brightly painted World War I biplane. Behind it the rising sun cast a pink glow over a grove of pecan trees.

Dew soaked through Bridget's canvas shoes as they made their way closer, through tall, pale-green grass. They stopped a few feet from the plane, and she simply stared, drinking it all in—the mists rising from the wet grass; the shiny, dew-dappled plane gleaming red, yellow and green; the pink and orange sky gradually giving way to blue.

"What do you think?"

She had no words to describe her awe. The scene he'd orchestrated was breathtaking, better than anything she could have imagined. All it lacked was him.

"Go stand by the plane," she said.

"Oh, but I'm not really—"

"Just do it."

"Okay." He walked over and stood in front of the plane's wing.

Bridget held up the thumb and forefinger of both hands, forming a rectangle in the air. She came closer, until Nick filled the frame, then backed away slightly so that she could see enough of the plane to identify it, and a bit of trees and sky in the background.

The light was the best part. That misty, early-morning light would make this portrait her masterpiece. That, and the subject himself. His had to be the most intensely interesting face she'd ever painted. So many facets to his personality. So many layers. As little time as she'd spent with him, she knew that about him.

"So, what do you think?" he asked impatiently, as if he was eager for her to approve.

She started to answer. Then she got a whiff of something—gasoline, motor oil. Her stomach roiled like an ocean during a hurricane. She held on to a brief hope that she could contain the nausea, then abandoned it. She was going to hurl.

She looked around frantically for somewhere to hide herself, but there wasn't a bush or tree within twenty yards. So she turned without explanation and fled toward the house, praying Nick wasn't the kind of man who locked his doors whenever he stepped outside.

Unfortunately she didn't make it as far as the house. She slid behind a wisteria bush and retched. There was nothing in her stomach, but she convulsed violently.

She heard Nick come up behind her and fervently wished the earth would swallow her up.

"Bridget?" His voice sounded full of concern, and at that moment she both hated and appreciated him. Appreciated him for caring. Hated him for seeing her like this, crouching in the bushes sicker than a dog. How humiliating!

"I'm fine, just give me a minute." She took several deep breaths and promptly passed out.

When she came to, probably only a few seconds later, she was being held in a pair of strong and utterly secure arms. She stifled the urge to insist that Nick put her down. For one thing she felt weak as a baby bunny, and she wasn't completely sure she could stand unless someone staked her up. For another it felt good to lie back and just let him take charge.

Nick was warm, and he smelled like the country and morning sunshine—the way her cotton clothes smelled if she dried them on a clothesline. She pressed her face against his shirt and closed her eyes again.

He didn't stop until he'd carried her all the way to his back porch, and then he paused only long enough to elbow the door open. Once inside, he set her down on a big, striped sofa as gently as if she were an armload of eggs.

She opened her eyes and blinked at him.

"Thank God. You're awake. Are you okay? What am I saying, of course you're not okay. You fainted." He ran his hands through his thick, chestnut hair.

Bridget thought irrelevantly that he was adorable when disconcerted.

"We should take you to the hospital," he announced.

She quickly found her voice. "No, really, that's not necessary. It's just morning sickness. By ten o'clock I'll be fine. Believe me."

"You fainted. I thought morning sickness was just nausea."

"I was light-headed. Maybe a little dehydrated."

"Eyes rolling into the back of your head is not 'light-headed.' You were unconscious."

"Just for a couple of seconds!"

"I'm calling a doctor. I have a friend—"

"No! As soon as I get something in my stomach, I'll be fine. And I have an appointment with my obstetrician this afternoon. I'll mention the morning sickness and see if he has any suggestions." She sat up, though it cost her to do it without groaning. "See, I'm feeling better already."

He looked almost convinced. She decided she'd better distract him with a task, or she'd be paying some strange doctor for a house call.

"Hot decaf tea with milk and honey usually helps. Do you have some tea?"

"No. Coffee?"

She shuddered. "'Fraid not."

"Orange juice?"

The thought of OJ made her stomach twinge. "A

glass of water and some dry toast or crackers?'' she countered.

''That I can do.''

He practically knocked over furniture in his effort to get to the kitchen. She could hear him clattering around in there, searching through drawers, opening and shutting cabinets. Heavens, didn't he know where things were in his own kitchen?

It occurred to her, then, that he might not live alone. He'd been at the charity ball without a date, and there clearly wasn't a woman in residence at the moment, or the panicked man would have dumped his ill guest on her. But maybe his wife traveled on business or something.

For the first time she took stock of his living room. Peach-and-white-striped furniture and pastel woven rag rugs created a pleasant atmosphere. A wealth of houseplants, set in decorative Mexican pots, were apparently thriving, probably due to the abundant light spilling in through two generous skylights. Either Nick had good taste, he'd hired a decorator or some woman had staked her claim on his home.

Then again, something about his house was uniquely male, even with the flowers out front and the pastel living room. It was...unpretentious, she supposed. Lived in. No fussy widgets on the coffee table or lace whats-its around the no-nonsense window blinds. He must be single, after all.

Just as well he was unattached, she decided. More than once she'd been doing a portrait for a husband, and the wife got jealous over the amount of time Bridget spent with the man.

She got up and took a closer look at the items on

his fireplace mantel—a large quartz crystal rock, a pocket watch under a display glass and a model biplane very similar to the one in the garden.

She nudged the tiny propeller on the plane, delighted to see it actually spun.

"I thought you were sick." Nick stood directly behind her, much too close for comfort.

She whirled around, her heart racing for no good reason. "It...comes and goes," she managed. "That's the way this morning sickness thing is."

He held a glass of ice water in one hand and a plate of buttered toast—at least four pieces—in the other. He'd forgotten she wanted it dry. He set both down on the maple coffee table. "Sit down before you fall down. A good breeze could blow you over."

She followed orders, not wishing to be any more of a problem than she'd already been. "I'm sorry if I scared you. I do appreciate your concern." She did, too, sort of.

Nick sank onto the opposite end of the sofa and put his head in his hands. Goodness, her sudden illness really had taken a lot out of the man.

"You're not going to sue me, are you?"

"Sue you? Good heavens, what for?" She nibbled on a corner of toast.

"I'm an easy target. And you were talking about suing my brother—"

"I never said I was going to sue your brother. I never even met your brother! That was my sister."

"She's pregnant, too?" he asked, faintly amused.

Bridget slumped back on the sofa. "No. She's not pregnant. She was referring to me, but she was only making a joke. Not a very good one, I'm—"

"A joke? I wouldn't think an unplanned pregnancy is something to joke about."

Now he was getting personal. "You think I should hide myself away like I've done something shameful?"

"Forgive me for saying so, but some people might think that sleeping with so many men that you don't even know your child's parentage is shameful. There, I've said it. I'm an old-fashioned, fossilized dinosaur. I know it. I can't help it."

Bridget knew she should be furious by the assumptions he'd made about her. But there was something pretty funny about a studly guy like Nick Raines talking about family values like a blue-haired old lady.

She folded her arms. "So, that's what this hostility is all about. It's not the baby that bothers you. It's my sleeping habits."

"It's both. I don't understand how you, a seemingly intelligent, successful woman, could so thoughtlessly conceive a child."

Okay. It was time to put that particular misconception to rest. "For your information, Nick—not that it's any of your business—I put a great deal of thought into conceiving this child. I love children. I want to raise a family more than anything in the world. I just don't happen to have a husband."

"How would you have time for a husband?" he grumbled.

What seemed humorous a moment ago suddenly didn't. Bridget felt tears coming on—her raging hormones had turned her into an emotional wreck—but she ruthlessly swallowed back the lump in her throat. "I was artificially inseminated."

She almost enjoyed the look of consternation on his handsome face. Then she promptly burst into tears.

"Oh...oh, here, now, stop that. There's no need..." Nick waved his hands around helplessly. "I'm sorry."

"It's okay," Bridget sniffed. "I'm just overemotional."

He held the glass of water out to her. "Here." When she didn't take it right away, he set it down, dashed out of the room, then back again with a box of tissues. "Here."

She took the tissue and dabbed at her eyes, then blew her nose in a most unladylike fashion. After a few more sniffs, she had herself under control.

"I'm really sorry," he said again, though he looked relieved. "I didn't mean to make you cry. But you have to admit, you did lead me to believe—"

"I didn't lead you anywhere. You assumed."

"I assumed the most likely scenario, given the limited information you gave me. I don't think I've ever known or even heard of a single woman having herself artificially inseminated."

"But you've known lots of women who slept around and got pregnant."

That stumped him for a moment. "Well, no. A couple in college, maybe."

Bridget took a deep breath. The crisis was over, and with it all of her hostility. Maybe she *had* deliberately led him to the unfair assumption. She was willing to let bygones be bygones if he was. "So, let's set up a schedule for our work together. Can you spare me an hour in the morning, three or four times a week for the next couple of weeks, then once a week thereafter?''

"You still want to do the portrait?''

"Yes, of course.''

"That's generous of you, considering I all but called you a slut.'' He almost let himself smile, and Bridget was reminded of exactly how handsome a man Nicholas Raines was, particularly when he wasn't showing off his sardonic wit at her expense.

"Can we please put the misunderstanding behind us and start fresh?''

"Okay. I think I can spare a few hours a week. I'll even buy some tea and honey and soda crackers, just in case.''

"Sounds like a plan.'' She stood up, feeling vastly better. "I think I should go home now.''

A couple of minutes later, as Nick opened Bridget's driver's door as if it were Cinderella's coach, she felt optimistic about the coming portrait. She always enjoyed committing a client's personality to canvas, but it had been a long time since a subject had so excited her creative juices. And maybe a few other types of juices as well.

"Just one more question,'' Nick said as he helped her into the car.

"Sure.''

"Don't you think your kid ought to have a father?''

Something in Bridget's imagination snapped shut. "A bit judgmental today, are we?''

"Just curious.''

Since the question hadn't been asked with the intention to antagonize, she decided to give him an honest answer. "I would dearly love for my child to have a father. But good husbands don't grow on trees. I've had several dating relationships over the past few years, but most of those guys, once I really got to know them, I couldn't picture as fathers. And the few 'maybes' flipped out if I even hinted at possible long-term goals."

"You mean they wigged when you said you wanted a baby."

"Something like that."

"Can you blame them? Most men aren't like women when it comes to children. They have to get used to being husbands first. Then they gradually grow into the idea of having kids."

"You know all about this, huh?"

"I know that if a lady I was dating suddenly started talking babies, I'd run as far and as fast as I could."

"You've just made my point for me." Bridget gave him a steely-eyed look. "I'm thirty years old. The old biological clock thing isn't just an old wives' tale."

"It's no fun growing up without a father," he said, making his point in a different way.

"What would you know about it? You were raised by Eric Statler, Jr."

"That's not exactly correct. My mother, who had me out of wedlock, by the way, met and married Statler when I was five. But he was never, ever my father."

Bridget realized she'd struck a sore spot. Nick's

feelings on this subject ran much deeper than she would have guessed. She felt for him. But the way he was raised had nothing to do with how she would bring up her child. She wouldn't allow any man into her life who didn't accept her son or daughter 100 percent.

"My sister and I were raised without a father, too," she said quietly. "Ours died when we were two and my mother never remarried. She loved us more than enough to make up for it. And we turned out okay."

"So it seems."

"For that matter, though you might regret some elements of your childhood, you seem to have turned out okay, too."

He sighed deeply. "Some might argue with you there."

"No family is perfect. But if you raise a child with love, whether you're one parent or two or ten, that has to be enough."

"I hope you're right." He was silent for a few moments, during which he seemed to close down. The bitter emotions flashing across his face faded until he could look at her impassively. "Tomorrow, same time?"

"Yes. That will be fine."

Bridget couldn't help thinking about their discussion during her drive home. There were lots of single mothers in the world. Some of them provided good homes for their kids; others didn't. Most of them hadn't chosen to raise kids by themselves, but somehow they coped, and the kids survived. Some thrived, like her and Liz. But what if she wasn't as good a mother as her own mother had been? What if the child, despite her hopes, wasn't good at coping with the stresses of a single-parent household?

Was it selfish and unfair of her, wanting to bring this child into the world without a father?

Nick Raines seemed to think so.

Chapter Four

"You are definitely showing," Liz observed as Bridget examined herself critically in the dressing room mirror.

Bridget sighed, plucking her loose-fitting denim dress away from her abdomen. "I was hoping this one would hide it a while longer, but I guess there's no denying it. I look pregnant. Time to put away the jeans and invest in some tent dresses."

"Hey, this is what you wanted, remember?" Liz groused. If *she* were pregnant, darn it, she would be flaunting it, not trying to hide herself away.

"Yeah, but the deal was, you and I were going to do it together. Look at you in those size six jeans. I wouldn't be able to get my big toe in those."

"Just wait a few months. I haven't given up," Liz said, studying a ragged fingernail. She pulled a nail file from her purse and went to work, casually adding, "I have a date tomorrow night with Ted."

Bridget gasped. "Ted, the gas station attendant at the corner by Mom's house?"

"Yeah, anything wrong with that? He's cute, and

he worships the ground I walk on. You're being an elitist."

Bridget unzipped the denim dress and stepped out of it, tossing it onto the "yes" pile. "I have nothing against a man who works with his hands for a living. However, I do think the father of your child should have an I.Q. a bit higher than an iguana's."

Liz snorted. "Find me one."

"You never like the suggestions I make."

"That's because your idea of a hot date involves poetry readings and sipping hot chocolate. Next time you set me up with a guy, would you at least check first to see if he has a pulse?"

"Okay, so maybe setting you up with my accountant wasn't such a hot idea." Bridget stepped into her jeans, which she couldn't snap, then pulled on a sweatshirt that hung almost to her knees. As she pulled on her sneakers, she paused and yawned. Twice.

"You okay, Bridge?" Liz asked, concerned by the shadows under Bridget's eyes. This pregnancy hadn't been easy for her. She was finally past the morning sickness, but she still seemed extremely fragile.

"Just tired, is all. I never realized how exhausting a baby could be before it's even born. I don't know how I'm going to make it to that party tonight."

Liz's senses went on alert. "Who's having a party that I didn't get invited to?"

"The costume party. I told you about it."

"That's tonight?" Liz had been pure green with envy when her twin had told her about the society party she'd been invited to.

"Yeah." Bridget just sat there.

"You don't seem very excited about it."

"I'm not. You know, my priorities have really changed. All I want to do is crawl into bed and sleep. Besides, I'll feel awkward. It was nice of Geraldine Statler to invite me, considering I've only met her once. She seems to have taken an inordinate amount of interest in the painting. But I doubt Nick wants me there."

"Oh, so it's *Nick* now, is it?" Seeing that Bridget didn't welcome any teasing, Liz backed off. "Funny, I could have sworn you liked him. You light up like a meteor shower every time you talk about him."

"Yeah, well, you're wrong. He thinks I'm a terrible person for having a baby with no father. He's cordial enough, but we're very tense around each other."

"Tension can have a lot of sources," Liz murmured.

Abruptly Bridget sat up straighter. "Hey, I've got a great idea. Why don't you go to the party in my place?"

"Bridget! We haven't pulled a switcheroo like that since college! Besides, the minute anyone sees me, they'll know I'm not you. I don't look like I swallowed a cantaloupe."

Bridget looked more animated than she had all day. "I'm not implying we should perpetrate a hoax. Just go to the party, introduce yourself to Geraldine Statler, and explain that you're my proxy. I guarantee she'll welcome you with open arms. She's very nice." Bridget gathered up the clothes she'd tried on, shouldered her purse and headed for the cash register.

"Uh-uh, no way. I'm not going near those Statler

people ever again." At the same time, Liz felt a little thrill at the idea of seeing Eric Statler up close once more. Ever since their ill-fated meeting at the Oilman's Ball, she'd devoured every news story she could find. She'd even gone to the Statler Enterprises Web site to gawk over pictures of Eric like an infatuated teenager.

"Chicken," Bridget murmured under her breath as she paid for her purchases.

"I am not. It's just…what kind of costume do you have?"

"I was planning to dig out my old Queen Elizabeth costume from when I was in that play in college, remember?"

"Hey, that's a great idea. All those yards of fabric will completely camouflage your stomach."

"Not my stomach," Bridget said, giving Liz's hair a playful tweak. "Yours."

Liz shook her head, even as she tried to picture herself decked out like a queen. "No way. I don't want to have to explain to Nick Raines why I'm not you."

"Nick won't come anywhere near you. He can hardly stand to be around me as it is."

Liz saw the hurt in Bridget's eyes and felt a pang of pity for her sister. Bridget had never been able to hide her feelings very well, and it was obvious from the way she talked about Nick that she had a thing for him, despite her protestations. Unfortunately, the guy was apparently a closed-minded jerk.

"I'll try on the costume," Liz finally said. "Just for fun, though. I'm not going to any party."

SEVERAL HOURS LATER, Liz found herself swathed in the most ridiculous brocade gown. The thing squashed her breasts so that they nearly spilled out of the stiff square neckline, and the skirt was so heavy she could barely walk. No wonder women were repressed back in the fifteenth century. They couldn't move.

Liz had been right about one thing. She could be ready to deliver a full-term baby under all that fabric and no one would know it.

She'd put a red rinse on her hair for a touch of authenticity. Then she'd added some pale makeup and painted on heavily arched brows. Even people who knew her wouldn't recognize her.

"Remember, introduce yourself to Geraldine Statler first," Bridget said, pressing the invitation into Liz's hand. "You won't have to do much more than say hi to her. She'll be much too busy for a long gabfest. I heard Nick is going dressed as a highwayman, so you can steer clear of him."

"I don't suppose you know what sort of costume Eric Statler will be wearing? *He's* the one I need to avoid."

Bridget shrugged. "I didn't ask."

"I can't believe you talked me into this. If you hadn't hit me with, 'The baby needs to rest...'"

"You'll have a blast. There are bound to be loads of eligible bachelors there. We're talking about the future father of my niece or nephew. I want you to choose wisely, and a larger sample of men can't hurt."

"Yeah, like I had a say in the father of *your* baby."

Bridget narrowed her eyes. "At least *my* baby's father won't be around to make my life miserable. What if Ted got you pregnant, then wanted to stick around? What if he wanted to marry you? Or, even worse, what if he sued you for custody?"

Liz's stomach took a sudden lurch. "Gee, I hadn't thought of that. If Ted got me pregnant, I could never tell him."

Bridget started hyperventilating. "Elizabeth Ann Van Zandt, you cannot steal a man's sperm without his consent. Whoever you pick as your 'donor,' you have to tell him about it. How would you like it if someone stole one of your eggs and made a baby without telling you? DNA is private property—"

"Okay, okay, put a hold on the rant. I wasn't really planning to get pregnant without telling the guy, whoever he might turn out to be. I just haven't gotten that far. I have to find a good candidate first. Then I'll come up with a strategy."

"This isn't a game, Liz. These are lives we're playing with. Don't do it lightly. Please."

Liz was taken aback by her sister's vehemence. Bridget had become much more emotional since her pregnancy, and Liz knew hormones were at least partly to blame. But something else was afoot.

"Bridget," she said, broaching the subject as cautiously as she knew how, "you're not regretting your pregnancy, are you?"

Bridget's face went all soft. "No, of course not. I love this baby so much it hurts, and I can't wait till I can hold him or her in my arms. But knowing that I've committed this kid to live without a father... I just want you to be fully aware of all the consequences, not just the good ones. Don't lose sight of the big picture.''

Liz gave Bridget a careful hug so as not to smear her makeup or ruin her hair. ''Don't worry—I won't.''

A horn tooted outside. Liz hadn't wanted to drive wearing the costume, so she'd called a cab. ''Wish me good hunting,'' she said as she grabbed her tiny evening bag and whisked out the door.

FOR ONCE IN HER LIFE, Liz felt completely out of place at a party. She didn't know a soul here at this huge, gaudy mansion. Normally that wouldn't have bothered her, but her ghastly performance at the Oilman's Ball was still fresh on her mind. The last thing she wanted to do was something embarrassing that would reflect badly on Bridget, who had shown extraordinary confidence in her by allowing her to come here at all.

She'd been looking everywhere for the party's hostess, to introduce herself, as Bridget had instructed. But Geraldine Statler was proving elusive.

Maybe if she just found an unobtrusive spot and watched the other guests cavort while she sipped the excellent champagne…which was exactly what Bridget would have done, except for the champagne part. For once, Liz decided, she was going to behave the way her more circumspect sister would have. She was not going to get herself in trouble.

''Would you like to dance, Elizabeth?'' a voice asked from behind her.

Liz's first panicked thought was that her deception had been uncovered. Then sanity returned, and she remembered the costume. She whirled around and found herself staring at a rather delicious-looking pirate. Long, curly dark hair cascaded out from under a red bandanna wrapped around his head like a football player's do-rag. Unfortunately, she couldn't tell much about his face. Though he didn't wear a mask, a thick black beard covered his cheeks and chin, and an eye patch left only one dark-brown eye visible.

It was the rest of him, though, that really caught her attention. He wore a leather vest over a bare, muscular torso. Baggy, striped pants, cut off at the knee, rode low on his lean hips. And he was barefoot.

"I'm not sure I can dance in this fifty-pound dress," she finally answered him.

"Sure you can, Your Highness," he said. "Just follow me."

Not giving her much chance to object, he led her through a doorway and into a ballroom—the Statlers had their own ballroom!—and onto a parquet floor, crowded with costumed revelers enjoying the country band.

Liz had always been a good dancer, but with the pirate she fairly floated across the floor. The brocade gown didn't hamper her at all, though she did catch herself glancing down at her neckline from time to time to be sure no more was showing than she intended.

"What's your name, queenie?" the pirate asked.

"Elizabeth, of course. Don't be cheeky to your betters."

"You're the cheeky one." With that he pulled her a bit closer than was entirely proper. Liz didn't care. His touch sent shivers coursing through her body.

She wasn't accustomed to having her arms around a half-naked man.

"What's your name?" she countered.

"Big Benny Blodgett."

"That's a car dealer in Dallas."

"Right, right." Then he murmured, "Knew I'd heard it somewhere. Are you having a good time?"

"Yes, delightful." She was about to tell him how she was attending the party in her sister's stead when the ballroom was plunged into complete darkness. The guitar amplifiers abruptly quit, too, and the band grated to a halt. Surprised, excited and frightened murmurs rose among the guests.

Liz instinctively grabbed on more tightly to her pirate. He hugged her to him.

"You're not afraid of the dark, are you?"

"Yes," she admitted, trying not to whimper. She was fearless when it came to just about anything— except this. When she was six, a neighborhood bully had locked her in a storm cellar and left her for two hours. In the inky blackness she'd imagined all sorts of horrible creatures crawling on her. She'd screamed herself hoarse until Bridget, wondering where Liz had gotten to, discovered her. Liz hadn't been able to abide the darkness ever since.

The pirate stroked her arm. "It's okay. Just a blown fuse. Happens all the time in this old house. I happen to know where the fuse box is. Wait right here for me."

"No!" Liz was ashamed by the neediness in her voice, but she couldn't abide being left alone. "I'll come with you."

"Okay." Deftly he led her through the milling

crowd, murmuring, "Excuse me, excuse me," while she clung to his arm. Flashlights and a candle or two had appeared, so the darkness wasn't as total as it had been.

Liz was completely disoriented, but her dance partner was heading unerringly for some destination.

"How do you know this place so well?" she asked, wondering if he worked here or something. Wouldn't Bridget get a kick out of the fact that Liz had come to the party to find herself a well-bred DNA donor, and instead she'd snagged the maintenance man?

"I lived here most of my life," he replied.

Liz decided not to press him further. If he was a servant, or the son of a maid or groundskeeper, perhaps it was better not to harp on it. He might be feeling a tad out of place among all these blue-blood swells—as she was.

She wondered what it would have been like growing up with Eric Statler. One thing for sure, the dark pirate might be good looking, but he was the opposite of blond Eric. He had a sense of humor.

They were walking on a tile floor now, Liz noted. A tiny bit of ambient light coming through a window reflected off a large, white surface. A refrigerator. They were in the kitchen.

The pirate opened another door, and Liz found herself in what felt like a closet of some kind. The door, on a spring hinge, closed behind them.

"Where are we?"

"Pantry." He fumbled around a moment until he found a small, metal door, then opened it. "There should be a flashlight in here somewhere...ah, here."

He flipped a switch, and a small flashlight came to life.

Liz took a deep breath. She was about to release her iron grip on the pirate when she noticed the light was fading. The flashlight's bulb grew dimmer by the second.

"Damn, most be old batteries," the pirate said.

Liz grabbed the flashlight. "No, no, no. You stay on!" She thumped it against the heel of her hand. Suddenly they were plunged into darkness again.

"Now you've done it," he said, just as she let out a little shriek and grabbed on to him again.

"I'm sorry," she said breathlessly. "I just hate the dark, I hate it, I hate it…" Liz realized she was damn close to hysteria. Yet the pirate's warm, virile presence eased her fears somewhat. He was so solid, and he smelled so good, like leather and beeswax.

"It's all right, Elizabeth," he crooned, stroking her shoulder, then her neck. "Nothing's going to happen to you. At least nothing bad."

She loved the sound of her name on his lips, even though he didn't know it was her real name. "I'm sorry," she murmured. "I'm such a baby."

"You feel all grown up to me." He wrapped his arm around her shoulders. Then he kissed her.

Amazing. One minute he'd been offering comfort, and the next he was kissing the daylights out of her. Her fear receded completely, and all she could think about was the feel of his mouth on hers, the way his hands felt hot even through the heavy brocade gown.

She had kissed her share of guys in her day, but no kiss had ever affected her like this. Her blood turned to warm wine rushing through her veins, intoxicating her, making her head spin. Her knees were tingling, and she knew if he let her go, she wouldn't be able to stand on her own.

"That is one crazy kiss you got there, Lizzy," he murmured against her hair. "You know, the whole time we were dancing, I kept looking at your mouth, wondering how it would taste."

"I was looking at your chest hair," Liz admitted, running her hands across his lightly furred pecs. Whatever she'd done, she'd inflamed him to action. He kissed her again, harder, and his hand somehow found its way to her breasts. It didn't take much effort to free one from her scandalous décolletage.

Was she out of her mind? Making out with a stranger in a pantry? She supposed she was, because she had no intention of stopping. Not yet, anyway. She'd connected with this man on some elemental level. Their cells were speaking to one another. She was hungry, starving for this man. It was like her body had recognized what it had been looking for her whole life.

ERIC COULDN'T BELIEVE he'd let the situation get this out of hand. He was kissing some strange woman in his parents' pantry, and things had progressed far past the necking stage. He had his hand down the front of her dress, and she was squeezing his butt.

Someone could walk in on them at any moment! He wasn't the only brilliant one in the family who knew where the fuse box was. If he were found groping a party guest whose name he didn't even know, his mother would faint, and he would find himself the object of gossip. Even worse would be Two's reaction. Though few would suspect it, Eric's father was one good shock away from another heart attack.

The very idea appalled him. Ever since the incident with his college girlfriend, Eric had spent all of his energy trying to live up to the exacting standards his father set, and by all accounts, so far he'd succeeded. In ten years he'd never created so much as a breath of scandal. He left that to Nick, who delighted in reading his name in a gossip column.

He knew he had to let go of this delectable woman. What if she was an employee? Or the wife of a client? What if she was married or—horrors!—underage?

That thought was like a bucket of cold water on him. Though he had a feeling this hot young woman would not have denied him all the pleasures of her body, he had to show some self-control. Determinedly he released her smooth, soft breast, pulled her questing hand away from his hindquarters and set them apart.

She made a small sound of protest.

"We can't," he said simply, his voice ragged with unmet desire. "I hear voices. Others will be coming this way."

Somehow he managed to grope around the fuse box without any light to guide him and find the main breaker switch. He could tell it had been tripped, probably by an overloaded circuit, so he flipped it back. Lights from the kitchen immediately shone under the door.

"That should do it. I'll leave first. Wait a couple of minutes, then slip out yourself. Okay? We don't want to get you in trouble."

"O-okay."

He grasped her chin, gave her one more quick, emphatic kiss, then left her.

A disoriented group of caterers stood in the kitchen, staring at him.

"All fixed," he said with a grin, then skirted past them. Mamie, his parents' cook, stared at him uncomprehendingly. She was probably wondering what a strange pirate was doing haunting the kitchen. She'd known him for twenty or more years, and even she didn't recognize him. Good. He got really tired of being Eric Statler III sometimes. He couldn't talk to anyone without his wealth standing between them, particularly women.

Now, take Queen Elizabeth, he thought with a wicked smile as he made his way back to the ballroom. Whoever she was, if she'd been aware of his identity, she probably wouldn't have responded to him as she had. She'd have been nervous. Or out to impress him. That was the first time he could remember a woman kissing him just because she liked his chest hair.

He would wait a few minutes, then try to find her again. And when he did, he would discover who she was.

Liz waited until the voices in the kitchen receded, then slipped out of the pantry herself. No one was about. She managed to find a powder room without encountering anyone, then almost fainted at what she saw. Her carefully applied makeup was smeared all over her face! Her right eyebrow had collided with her lipstick somewhere in the middle of her cheek.

One false eyelash was hanging by a thread. Her red-tinted hair had come loose from the elaborate head-dress and hung in disorganized ringlets.

The queen had turned into a witch, and a really scary one at that.

She had to get out of here. But how could she escape unnoticed? Anyone who saw her would know exactly what she'd been up to. She spotted a Japanese fan hanging on the wall. Perfect. She would slip through the main hall, the fan hiding her face, then give the fan to one of the valets as she climbed into a cab.

Her heart sank as she thought about her pirate. No chance to waylay him and wiggle a name or phone number out of him. Rats, he probably wasn't available, anyway, she mused uncharitably as she checked the hallway, then darted back to the kitchen. Why else would he have been so mortified at the idea of being seen alone with her?

"ARE YOU ENJOYING YOURSELF?" Nick's mother asked him. "You look very dashing in that costume."

"I feel like an idiot," he groused. "I'd only wear this ridiculous getup for you."

Geraldine Statler, dressed as a geisha, put her arm around her oldest son and hugged him to her—no small feat, since he was a good foot taller than her. "I'm very pleased and surprised you came at all. You haven't attended one of my Halloween parties since you were ten."

"Then I guess it's high time."

He wasn't sure why he'd decided to cave in and

attend the party, in costume no less. He didn't want to examine his motives too carefully, either. He was sure his decision had nothing to do with the fact that a certain alluring portrait artist would be in attendance.

"Have you seen Ms. Van Zandt yet?" Geraldine asked casually.

Nick shivered. His mother could read him too accurately sometimes. "No, I haven't. Then again, it's hard to recognize anyone tonight."

"I haven't seen her, either. I was curious what costume she would wear. She's so very pretty, don't you think?

His mom was fishing. She'd gotten it into her head to play matchmaker, but Nick was having none of it. "She's okay."

"Is that her in the harem outfit?" Geraldine nodded discretely toward a group standing a few feet away.

Nick laughed. Bridget in a harem outfit? He doubted it. "No, that's not her," he said, shaking his head. "She's pregnant."

Geraldine frowned. "Oh, so she's married."

"No, she's not. She's chosen to have a baby out of wedlock." And, because he didn't want his mother to make the same mistake he'd made, he added, "She was artificially inseminated."

Geraldine's eyebrows shot up, but after a moment she smiled. "That's a brave decision. Goodness, I wish she'd talked to me first. Though in this day and age, people pay no mind to single mothers anymore. Not like when I had you." She paused to carefully sip from her glass of champagne so as not to muss her makeup. "Well, good for her. I hope it works out."

And that, Nick thought smugly, would end Geraldine's machinations. She could hardly promote a match between her son and an unwed mother. Nick's stepfather, Two, would not be a happy camper.

"Oh, my gracious, would you look at that," Geraldine said, pointing toward an elaborately gowned redhead scurrying through the front hall and making for the door. "She's got my Japanese fan!"

Nick took off after the thief at once. The fan, which had hung in the powder room for as long as Nick could remember, was over a hundred years old and very valuable.

He caught up with the woman just as she was waving at a cab driver. He grabbed her arm and lowered it, revealing the face that had been hidden by the fan.

"Bridget?"

Her face was smeared with makeup almost beyond recognition. It was quite apparent what she'd been up to, and why neither he nor his mother had spotted her. She'd found herself some stud and had been having her way with him—under his mother's roof!

"Um, Nick?"

"What exactly are you doing with my mother's fan?"

"I was going to return it," she said peevishly. "It must be fairly obvious I was trying to hide my face, since I'm somewhat…in disarray."

"That's one way to put it."

She snapped the fan shut and handed it to him. "Here. I really have to go." Looking distressed, she hopped into the cab and slammed the door.

Nick let her leave. Her comings and goings were none of his business. At least, they shouldn't be. He and Bridget had a business relationship, nothing more. The fact that she wasn't as prim and conservative as she seemed ought not to concern him at all.

But it did, damn it.

A dastardly looking pirate sprinted out the front door. "Elizabeth?" he called, looking frantically all around. Then he spotted Nick. "Hey, Nick, did you see Queen Elizabeth come out here just now?"

Nick just stared for a moment. "Eric? Good God, what have you done to yourself?" His face was covered by a scraggly black beard, half peeling off.

"Did you see her?"

"She just left in a cab."

Eric's face fell. He pulled off the kerchief and fake black curls, and ran his fingers through his own blond, expensively cut hair. He removed the eye patch, too, revealing one blue and one brown eye. He'd gone all out with this costume thing, to the point of wearing a brown contact lens.

"Damn," Eric said. "Do you know her?"

Nick noted the unmistakable smears of white makeup clinging to the shreds of Eric's fake beard.

Perfect. Just perfect. It figured Eric would be the one. "No, I don't believe I know her," Nick lied.

Chapter Five

"Turn just a bit to the right, please, Nick," Bridget said.

Nick, who'd been patiently following her directions for the past fifteen minutes as he stood next to his biplane in the early morning light, suddenly exploded.

"I've turned to the right. I've turned to the left. I've moved my feet. I've moved my hands. I've smiled. I've frowned. What is it with you this morning? Why can't you get it right?"

A lump grew in Bridget's throat. Darn hormones again. She cried at the drop of a hat these days.

"I'm sorry!" she said, throwing down her brush. "Maybe it's the changing seasons, but the light doesn't seem the same." And Nick didn't seem the same, either. During their last portrait session a couple of weeks ago, he'd been much warmer toward her. He'd teased her about her perfectionist tendencies, and he'd actually asked her how far along her pregnancy was and whether she knew yet whether it was a boy or a girl. Most people stared determinedly away from her stomach and didn't mention it.

She'd thought a thaw was coming on. But today she and Nick were back to square one. He was restless as a caged hawk, and she sensed he was about to bolt.

And could she blame him? This portrait had taken three times as long as any other she'd painted. Summer was giving way to fall—she'd had to wear a jacket this morning. The trees in the background were changing from green to yellow and gold, and the north wind had a definite bite to it.

"If you can just bear with me for another ten minutes, I'll be done for the day," she promised.

"You said that ten minutes ago."

"My, aren't we peevish this morning," she said, hoping to tease him out of his rotten mood. "Get up on the wrong side of bed?"

"Maybe so, but at least it was my own bed."

Bridget thought perhaps she hadn't heard right. "What did you just say?" she asked sharply.

"Nothing. Forget it."

"I don't want to forget it. And you can stop posing. I can't paint you when you're staring at me like a glacier. What did you say?"

"I said, 'at least it was my own bed.' The comment was in poor taste, and I apologize."

"Poor taste!" Bridget rose from her camp stool, vibrating with fury. "That's an understatement. I thought we'd settled this issue of my sleeping habits some time ago." She could not imagine what had prompted this new attack on her morals.

"That was before the party. Look, you're right, it's none of my business. An old sibling rivalry rears its ugly head, that's all. It isn't the first time a woman used her acquaintance with me to get to my brother.''

Bridget's head hurt. ''I have no earthly idea what you're talking about. If you think I weaseled an invitation out of your mother—''

''I don't have an issue with your attending the party. It's your behavior at the party that irked me, though it probably shouldn't.''

''Oh, no.''

Mistaking her horrified utterance for a denial, he continued relentlessly. ''I'm not blind. I saw you, *Queen Elizabeth,* with your makeup smeared and your hair all mussed.''

Bridget made a noise that was half yelp, half shriek of outrage. ''It was Liz, my twin,'' she blurted out.

''Ah, yes, the evil twin. We all have one of those, don't we? You're lucky my mother didn't want to press charges about the fan. It's very valuable.''

''What fan?''

''The one you were trying to make off with. That's not a very nice way to repay her kindness—''

''Will you be quiet!'' Bridget roared in a very unBridgetlike voice. ''There, now, that's much better. I'm trying to tell you something. I wasn't feeling well the night of the party, so my twin sister, Liz, went in my place.''

Nick was shaking his head. ''Nice try. You spoke to me, remember?''

Bridget was going to kill her sister. Liz had been unusually mum about the party, claiming it had all been a big bore and she'd gone home early.

Well, Bridget had had enough of trying to explain about her sister's scandalous behavior. A real, live, breathing identical twin ought to be worth a thousand words. She pulled the cell phone from her pocket—she carried it with her at all times now, in case of a medical emergency—and dialed her sister's home number. Fortunately she caught Liz before she left for work.

"Liz, I need you."

Liz gasped. "The baby? Is something wrong—"

"No, nothing like that. I need you to drive out to Nick Raines's house and prove to him I have a twin. He doesn't believe me."

"I can't. I'll be late for work."

"Well, then, I guess I'll just have to talk with Mrs. Statler about a certain fan—"

"I'll be there in fifteen minutes. Give me the directions."

NICK WATCHED in stunned silence during Bridget's one-sided conversation. Was it possible she really did have a twin? She'd mentioned her "evil twin" on the first day she'd come to Peachy's Air Freight, but he'd thought it was a joke.

As Bridget began packing away her art supplies, Nick started helping, as had become their custom. But she gave him a look so scathing that he shrank back. Good gravy, he'd really stepped in it this time.

What had gotten into him? He'd had a couple of weeks since the party to stew over what he saw, and the more he'd thought about it, the more indignant he'd become. By this morning he'd convinced himself that Eric and Bridget were carrying on a torrid affair behind his back, that Bridget had used her connection to him, and then to Geraldine, to get to Eric and work her wiles on him.

But if there was a twin… Could she be telling the truth?

"Liz should be here in five or ten minutes," Bridget said as she slammed the trunk lid on her car a few minutes later. "Don't even think of ducking out before she gets here. I want you to hear what she has to say. Then I'll expect an apology."

"Can I apologize now instead? It wasn't my place to judge—"

"No. I don't want any more of your *generous* tolerance of my less-than-sterling character. I want a full-blown, groveling, on-your-knees apology for repeatedly calling me easy. And if I don't get it, I'm going to put my foot through that canvas in my trunk, and I will pay you back every cent of your five grand even if I have to take out a second mortgage."

Nick felt himself growing weak at the prospect of her destroying all the weeks of work, his and hers, that had gone into the portrait so far. "Don't do that, Bridget. Really. There's no need. You'll get your apology. Want some coffee?" he added lamely.

"Caffeine's bad for the baby."

Thankfully, they didn't have to wait much longer. A red Miata came roaring down the driveway a couple of minutes later, squealing to a stop mere inches from them. The driver's door opened, and a lovely blond woman in a hot-pink business suit with matching pumps stepped out.

She was, indeed, Bridget's double, right down to the hairstyle. Only her slender waistline distinguished her from her sister.

Nick gulped a few times, but no words came out.

The newcomer came toward him and extended her hand. "Hi, Nick, I'm Liz Van Zandt."

He shook her hand as Bridget looked on smugly. "I believe I've already had the pleasure."

"Twice, actually. Once at the Oilman's Ball and again at the costume party."

Of course! That's why his observations of "the Van Zandt woman" had seemed so odd at the Oilman's Ball—attraction waxing and waning till his head had spun. He'd been drawn to both of their looks, of course, since they were identical. But it was Bridget's quiet flirtation—if it could even be called that—that had really reeled him in.

A wave of relief washed over him. Liz was the one who'd been messing around with his brother, not Bridget. That situation was rife with its own humor, and he would explore it later. Right now he had to focus on mending fences with Bridget.

He turned to her. "I don't know what to say."

"An apology would be nice."

"When you mentioned your evil twin, I thought—"

"Evil!" Liz interrupted. "Bridget, what have you been telling him?"

"I thought it was just a joke. You know," Nick continued doggedly. "An expression."

"Even so," Bridget said, arms and ankles crossed, gaze averted in body language a two-year-old could read. "What if it *had* been me at the party, flirting with your brother?" She shot an accusing glance at Liz.

"I did *not* flirt with his brother!" Liz objected.

Bridget ignored her and continued staring knives at Nick. "Does that give you the right to treat me like—"

"A flirt?" Nick said, then laughed humorlessly. "It was a little more serious than that. And let's not forget about the fan."

"I wasn't trying to steal that fan," Liz interjected. "I'd smeared my makeup badly, and I borrowed the fan so I could get to the taxi without people staring. I was going to give the fan to one of the valets to return."

Bridget gasped. "Liz! Taking something without permission is not 'borrowing.'"

"I was desperate," Liz said.

"And how exactly did your makeup get so smeared?" Bridget asked suspiciously.

Liz's expression turned downright mulish. "That's none of your business, but I swear to you, it had nothing to do with Eric Statler."

"Whatever!" Bridget said impatiently. "It doesn't matter whom you were throwing yourself at this time. It's not really any of *his* business, is it?" She pointed at Nick.

"It is if he has a crush on you," Liz said with an impish smile.

"Grown men do not have crushes," Nick objected, though Liz had hit a bit closer to home than he'd like to admit. What he felt for Bridget *was* something akin to a crush—an unrequited, unexpressed yearning for a woman he could never, in a million years, get involved with.

Bridget just looked disgusted with the whole argument. Good. He'd managed to keep his burgeoning lust for her under wraps, and that was the way it would remain. *Pregnant women are off-limits,* he reminded himself.

"I'm leaving," Bridget announced.

"Same time next week, Bridget?" he called after her, trying to assume an air of normality. Maybe, given the odd circumstances, she would see fit to overlook his earlier boorish behavior.

Her mouth thinned into a tight line. "I don't believe I'll need you to sit for me any longer, Nick. With the seasons changing, the light and the background are all wrong, anyway. I can finish up the painting using the photos."

Nick felt like he'd just been stabbed in the heart. Though he'd proclaimed the portrait sittings a nuisance to anyone who would listen, he'd gotten used to them. He'd started to look forward to them. Wednesday mornings just wouldn't be the same without Bridget fussing at him to comb his hair or drop his chin or shift his gaze a fraction of an inch to the left.

He would also miss feeling her lively gaze on him. The way she'd studied every nuance of his face and body had given him an erotic thrill.

"Well, that's a relief," he lied.

"Yes, I'm sure you can find better things to do with your Wednesday mornings."

Not really, he caught himself thinking.

Both women started to get into their cars, but Liz took her time. After Bridget's car door closed securely, Liz turned to Nick. "Bridget shows her affection for a man in strange ways."

Then both twins were gone, and Nick felt bereft.

Without the portrait sittings, he had no excuse in the world to see Bridget. He'd thought he would welcome having her out of his hair. She'd been nothing but trouble, disrupting his schedule and stirring up his hormones. But his heart was heavy.

BRIDGET WASN'T ABOUT to let Liz slither away to work. Her behavior at the Statlers' party demanded a full explanation. And Nick wasn't the only one who owed her an apology. She pulled her cell phone out of her skirt pocket, turned it on and hit the speed dial button for her sister's car phone.

Liz answered immediately. "Liz Van Zandt."

"Meet me at Truelove's," Bridget said tightly.

"Oh, it's you. Thought it might be my boss calling. I'm already twenty minutes late—"

"Call your office and tell them you've been delayed by a…a health problem."

"But I don't have a health problem," Liz objected.

"You will—like maybe a broken elbow—after I get done with you."

"Oh, okay, I can get a cup of coffee and a bagel. I skipped breakfast because of you."

Bridget flipped off her phone before she said something she'd regret.

LIZ TRIED TO GET all her ducks in a row before pulling into the parking lot at Truelove's, her and Bridget's favorite diner. Had she really done anything that unforgivable? Was she bound to reveal every detail of her life to Bridget just because she'd used Bridget's invitation to get to the masquerade party?

Well maybe she was, Liz thought, turning off her

convertible's engine. She had known Nick mistook her for Bridget, and she'd done nothing to correct his misconception. Then she'd deliberately been vague when Bridget had asked her about the party. But explaining about the smeared makeup and the fan would have necessitated an explanation about the pirate, and she wasn't quite ready to do that. Her pantry rendezvous had been more than an impulsive and daring stunt. She'd felt an attraction to the man that was unlike anything in her experience. She had connected to him, and she was sure he'd felt a similar bond. She knew it just from the way he'd held her, the way he'd murmured her name in that husky voice.

Liz's face heated at the memory.

Bridget pulled into the space next to Liz, climbed out and nodded tersely toward the diner's front door. With a sinking stomach, Liz followed. She was in for one of Bridget's lectures, and maybe this time she even deserved it.

Truelove's was all red vinyl and turquoise Formica—not retro, but the genuine article. It had opened in the fifties and, since Liz could remember, had served all manner of traditional, fattening breakfasts like bacon and eggs, pancakes with real butter, biscuits and sausage gravy. But when Jenny Truelove had taken it over a few years ago, she'd updated the menu to include bran muffins, bagels and gourmet coffee to compete with some of the new specialty restaurants and designer chains moving in.

"Hey, twins," Jenny called from behind the cash register. "Just sit anywhere, the breakfast rush is over."

Bridget smiled in acknowledgment, then resumed her scowl and led the way to a booth in the back corner. She said nothing until the pink-uniformed waitress had taken their orders—herbal tea and a muffin for Bridget, and coffee with a raisin bagel for Liz.

"You're gonna starve that kid," Liz said, nodding toward Bridget's tummy.

"Don't change the subject."

"I didn't know there was a subject."

"What, exactly, happened at that party?" Bridget grated out.

"Not what Nick made it sound like. I was dancing with this gorgeous pirate—"

"Not Eric Statler?"

"I never even laid eyes on Eric Statler, okay? Nick must have been hallucinating that part. The guy I was with had long, dark, curly hair, brown eyes and a full beard. You know, a pirate."

"When you say you were 'with' him—"

"Would you stop interrogating me? There was a power failure, and the dark scared me a little, so I grabbed on to the pirate. Next thing you know, we were kissing."

"And that's all?"

"Not that it's any of your business, but yes, that's all. Much as I'd like to be impregnated, even I wouldn't make love with a complete stranger at a party to which I wasn't really invited."

"It's my business when Nick and his mother think you're me!"

"Well, they don't anymore, okay? We got that straightened out."

The waitress arrived with their orders. Liz fell on her bagel like a wolverine. She was starving. Bridget picked at her muffin.

"I'm sorry my behavior caused a problem between you and Nick," Liz finally said.

"It's okay," Bridget said on a sigh. "It's not like *that* was going anywhere."

"Would you want it to?"

"No! That is, it would never...we're all wrong—"

"I was right. You have a thing for him."

Bridget sighed again. "Yeah," she said simply.

"So why'd you cut him off at the knees?"

"I've already dragged this portrait thing out twice as long as I needed to. The painting is all but done."

"So? Invent another excuse to see him."

"I can't. I'm pregnant, remember?"

"Some men find pregnant women terribly attractive."

"He just finds me terrible."

"Oh, sister, you are wrong about that. That man is smitten."

Bridget snorted. "He thinks I'm morally reprehensible for bringing a child into the world without a father."

"Since when did a woman's perceived lack of morals hurt her chances with a guy?"

Bridget waved away Liz's argument. "Forget it. It's over, I'm done with Nicholas Raines. I have more important things to concentrate on than snagging a boyfriend. Anyway, I want to hear more about this pirate."

Liz welcomed the chance to unburden herself.

She'd been keeping it inside for so long. "He was gorgeous. And he had a great sense of humor. He was a good dancer and an even better kisser."

"And does this pirate have a name?"

"No. I mean, yes, of course, everyone has a name, but he didn't see fit to give it to me. Unless Big Benny Blodgett is his real name."

"That three-hundred-pound guy who sells Chevys on late-night TV?"

"It wasn't him," Liz said firmly. "Actually, I think he might be a maintenance worker on the Statler estate. He knew right where the fuse box was."

Bridget chuckled. "A house full of doctors and lawyers, and you snag the maintenance man."

"Don't be a snob."

"Oh, I'm just teasing. I'm sure he's a perfectly wonderful guy. It's really awful you didn't get his name."

Liz sat back smugly and folded her arms. "I'm going to find him, Bridget. I've already put a plan in motion."

Bridget's eyes narrowed. "What kind of plan?"

Liz grinned. "Take the Interstate south on your way home."

"That would be out of my way."

"Do it, anyway. You'll see what I mean." Liz glanced at her watch. "Oh, damn, I've got to get out of here or my miserable excuse for a boss will fire me." She threw a five-dollar bill on the table and scooted out of the booth. She didn't want to answer any more questions about her quest for the pirate. Bridget would find out soon enough, and Liz didn't want to be around when she did.

BRIDGET PAID THE CHECK, walked out into the November sunshine, and climbed into her car. What was crazy Liz talking about now? Bridget was too tired and too disheartened to give it much thought. But she did take the highway home, just in case there was anything remarkable.

Remarkable was an understatement. Liz was so shocked when she saw it that she had to pull over to the shoulder and catch her breath.

A huge billboard—the biggest one on the whole darn highway—carried a message: Sir Pirate, Queen Elizabeth Awaits Your Pleasure.

Her brazen sister had propositioned a man in two-foot-high letters!

Chapter Six

Liz had never spent such a long day at work. It was only eight hours, like any other day, but she'd been so distracted even her normally insensitive boss had asked her what was wrong.

"My sister's mad at me," was all she could think to say, which was true enough. Bridget had called her, after seeing the billboard, and given her another lecture. But Liz wasn't about to explain to her employer that she was beside herself with anxiety over a billboard and its anticipated results.

Would her pirate call? she wondered on her drive home. What if he never even saw the billboard? Or what if he saw it and decided his "Elizabeth" must be a loony tune to go to so much trouble to find some guy she'd danced with at a party?

All in all her chances of actually connecting with the guy in some positive way were almost nil. As Bridget had pointed out, Liz had probably wasted a lot of money on that billboard, even with her ad agency discount.

But she'd had to do something. It was crazy, but that whole encounter with the pirate had meant something to her. She'd never believed in fate or luck or Kismet, but when that guy had dropped into her life, she'd felt, for a few brief minutes, that the gods had smiled on her.

Her hand trembled as she dialed the phone of her new answering service. Was Bridget right? Was she out of her mind to put a provocative message on a billboard, along with a phone number?

At least she hadn't put her home phone out on the freeway, she reasoned. The answering service assured her complete anonymity, so she never had to talk to any of the annoyance callers she was sure to get.

"You have—" the automated voice told her "—sixty-four messages."

Liz nearly dropped the phone. Sixty-four? *Sixty-four?* Hot dog, she knew what she was doing tonight. Listening to a bunch of crazy, horny guys, probably.

She settled onto the sofa with a notebook and began listening to the messages. As each new one started she held her breath, only to release it in an exasperated sigh when she immediately recognized that the voice was all wrong.

"Hey, if this is a new dating service," an eager male voice said on message number ten, "I want in. You got a sexy voice, Elizabeth. Call me at…" Liz hit the three button on her phone to advance to the next message.

"I'm not a pirate, but I'm rich," number eleven informed her. "I'm a pro football player, yeah, and, um, Donald Trump's nephew. Call me at…"

Number thirteen was a heavy breather. Number seventeen made a suggestion so disgusting Liz's face burned, even though she was alone in the room.

Twenty-four sounded like he was thirteen years old. He wanted to know her bra size, and would she meet him after school? Twenty-seven was a woman who told Elizabeth she didn't need to degrade herself to find a man, and if she would join this certain feminist support group she would learn to live happily without men.

"Fat chance," Liz muttered, hitting the three button.

Thirty-two actually sounded nice, as if maybe he wasn't an ax murderer or an escapee from a mental institution. Under other circumstances she might have been intrigued, but today she had ears only for her pirate.

By message sixty-three she was beginning to lose heart. Maybe today wasn't the day. The billboard would be up another forty-eight hours. If Mr. Pirate didn't personally see it, surely someone would mention it to him.

With a sinking heart she hit the button to listen to the last message, and there he was. Again she almost dropped the phone.

"Elizabeth, it's me, um, Big Benny. I don't normally do this kind of thing..."

"Oh, me, neither," Liz said, as if he could hear her. She pressed the phone to her ear, wanting to bring him closer.

"...but, what the heck. I'll be at the Cliff House Hotel all day tomorrow, but I think I can sneak away for a few minutes in the afternoon. Around two? Meet me in the lobby."

That was it. No phone number, no real name, no

way to contact him should two o'clock tomorrow be inconvenient. He was awfully sure of himself.

She'd practically been given a royal summons. And she was supposed to be the queen! It would serve him right if she didn't show up.

But she knew there was no way she could stay away. At the very least she had to know what he looked like in normal attire. Did he work at the hotel? she wondered. Or maybe he was there for a meeting.

She laughed at herself. With that long hair and beard, he wasn't some executive in wing tips and a double-breasted suit. She couldn't get her hopes up that this guy was a romantic match for her. She wanted his DNA, pure and simple. She would talk with him, casually find out his medical and family history. And if she still deemed him good father material, she would put the question to him.

Would he father her child, no strings attached?

How could he resist such an offer? Men had a hard time turning down free, no-commitment sex.

ERIC WAS BEGINNING to seriously doubt his judgment. "Queen Elizabeth" had taken out a personal ad—on a billboard, for all of Oaksboro to see—and he'd swallowed the bait. If word ever got out that he'd done such a damn fool thing as dial a woman's number off a billboard, he would be a laughingstock. The reporters, who'd spent years digging into his past, unsuccessfully trying to find some small indiscretion to magnify, would pounce on this tidbit like pigs on an apple core.

But he hadn't yet reached the point of no return, he reasoned as he stifled a yawn at this interminable business lunch with the manager of Cliff House. The small, luxury hotel was one of Statler Enterprises' holdings, and today was Eric's annual "meet and greet" with the management and staff to check up on things.

This morning he'd met with employees to hear suggestions for improving operations and air grievances. He always enjoyed that part. The maids, bellboys and desk clerks seemed to value his interest in their jobs, and they never failed to come up with at least one good idea. Before lunch he'd consulted with an electrical engineer about an elevator that was always getting stuck. This afternoon would be devoted to inspecting the physical property itself, to see that the hotel was being kept up to the standards he demanded.

During lunch, he had to listen to his officious manager, Dalton Graham, complain about insignificant problems. The man ran this hotel with military efficiency, and the employees seemed to like him, but Eric found his whining a real annoyance.

Especially today.

Eric surreptitiously checked his watch again. One forty-five. In fifteen minutes Queen Elizabeth would stroll through the hotel's front door, and he intended to be ready for her.

Although they'd both been in costume at the party, he had the advantage. He had some idea of what her facial features were, despite all the makeup. Her eyes were a spectacular blue, he recalled, and her lips were lush and full. And she would be alone, waiting for someone.

He, on the other hand, would be virtually unrecognizable. And he could stand around chatting with the desk clerks. He could check her out beforehand and decide whether he would go through with the meeting.

It would be a trifle cruel not to meet her, after he'd asked her here. But a man in his position had to protect himself. Once she knew his true identity, she had power over him. She could blab to reporters about his pantry indiscretions and the fact that he'd called a number on a billboard to locate her. He had to decide, based on appearance alone, whether he could trust her with that power.

Fortunately, he was a master at evaluating people based on their appearance, clothing, hairstyle, and body language.

At ten minutes to two, Eric cut short Dalton's harangue about the rising cost of fresh flowers for the lobby. "I'll have someone on my staff research the area florists and see if we can't come up with a better deal," he said. "But I really have to go."

"But the facility tour doesn't start until two-thirty," Dalton objected, obviously hoping for another thirty minutes to bend Eric's ear.

"If you have any other concerns, put them in a memo," Eric told him, getting up from his chair. "Please compliment Raoul on an excellent lunch."

The nugget of praise seemed to placate Dalton. Eric made his escape.

The lobby was full of women when Eric emerged from the restaurant. Then he remembered: the hotel was hosting a two-day cosmetologists' convention. Stylish ladies of all ages with lots of makeup and good manicures were milling about the lobby, socializing, comparing notes from the morning session, making dinner plans. How would he ever find Elizabeth in this mess?

Then he saw her, a woman standing alone, looking out the front window. Her back was to him, but he could see she was slender and that she carried herself with a certain regalness. Her honey-blond hair fell loose to her shoulders in a simple style, yet he could tell she had an expensive salon cut. Her clothes, too—black pants and a gold linen jacket—had a certain stylish elegance to them that spoke of taste and refinement.

Well, duh, he thought. He'd met the woman at his mother's party, and Geraldine's friends tended to be wealthy. She could be the rich daughter of one of her friends, or someone she worked with on a charity committee. Or she could be the pool man's daughter. His mother wasn't a snob, and she still maintained many connections from her pre-Statler days.

Eric didn't know how he came to the decision, but some instinct told him this woman was okay. She was probably as sensitive to scandal as he was. He would at least talk to her.

He strode purposefully toward her, but he stopped a couple of feet behind her, inhaling her breezy perfume.

Nice. He could stand to breathe a whole lot more of it. He touched her gently on the shoulder. "Excuse me—"

She whirled around, startled. Damn, Eric thought, the woman was not just pretty, she was gorgeous. Not only that, but she looked distinctly familiar. He'd met her somewhere other than his mother's party, he was sure of it. He racked his brain for when and where, but couldn't quite come up with it, which was unusual. Normally his memory catalogued names and faces like a computer.

She stared at his face. Then her mouth dropped open, and her eyebrows arched up almost as high as the ones she'd painted on the other night.

"Eric Statler?" she squeaked.

He nodded. Uh-oh. She was going to be one of those who couldn't separate him from his public image. He felt a palpable disappointment, and he experienced a fleeting wish for that pirate costume. He'd had no idea how much fun it would be to shed his true identity.

"I'm not here to cause you any trouble, I promise," the woman said, backing away from him. "I didn't even know you were going to be here. I'm meeting a…a friend here. Honestly. Please don't kick me out."

"Kick you…what?" Then it struck him where he'd met her. The Oilman's Ball in this very hotel. She'd been babbling something then, too, about her sister being pregnant and his being responsible. Even after he'd pointedly told her to go away, she'd approached him again. Regrettably, he'd had her thrown out of the ballroom.

"I'll sit very quietly here in this corner until my…friend shows up," she said, her blue eyes pleading with him to show mercy. "Then I'll leave, I promise."

Eric almost burst out laughing at the ridiculousness of it all. His dream woman, his Elizabeth of the angelic eyes and wicked kisses, was the crazy lady from the Oilman's Ball who'd wanted to slap a paternity suit on him?

Fate was too cruel.

And what game was she playing this time? He wanted no part of it. He was about to tell her so, in no uncertain terms, when the meaning of her words struck him like a two-by-four. She'd said she was meeting someone. She was looking for her pirate. She didn't recognize him. She hadn't caught on.

"Calm yourself, ma'am," he said in a soothing voice. "You can stay here and meet your friend. I thought you were someone else." Like perhaps someone he had a small chance of compatibility with?

"Oh, thank you. You've very kind. The incident at the Oilman's Ball—"

"The less said about that, the better."

"Right. Not another word."

"Well. All right, then." For some reason Eric was loath to walk away from her. She was very pretty, true, but he had his pick of pretty women. But she was different, somehow. She seemed so genuine. She wouldn't know how to simper or make idle chitchat over cucumber sandwiches if she had to. He was really tired of the debutantes and heiresses he often took as escorts to this function or that. Their banter was so well rehearsed. There was no spontaneity, especially around him.

He forced himself to nod a farewell and turn away from her. Then he had to think about cold showers and liverwurst so as not to embarrass himself. He couldn't remember ever having had such a visceral reaction to a woman.

He returned to his conversation with one of the clerks, going over the new computer record-keeping system and the ways she thought it might be improved.

"I've taken some computer programming classes down at the junior college," she said, obviously trying not to sound too eager. Her name was Miranda, and she was barely out of high school. "I could take a crack at fixing the problem. With your permission. Sir."

"Yes, by all means," he said distractedly. His attention was on the blond woman, whose name he still didn't know, though he continued to think of her as Queen Elizabeth. She'd stopped looking out the window and was now seated in one of the lobby's plush sofas, small hands clasped in her lap.

She didn't look nearly as self-possessed as she had when he'd first spotted her. And why should she? It was nearly 2:15. She'd been stood up. That wasn't good for any woman's ego.

She ought to be spitting mad, he mused. Instead she looked forlorn. Damn. He couldn't live with himself if he left her like that. "Excuse me, Miranda."

The cosmetologists had all gone to their afternoon sessions, so the lobby was nearly empty now. He made his way over to her. Her gaze darted back and forth between the front door, the door to the restaurant and the elevators. She didn't see him approaching until he was nearly on her.

She jumped. "Just a few more minutes and you'll never see me again, I promise."

And wouldn't that be a shame, he caught himself thinking. "Your, um, friend didn't show up?"

"No, I guess not," she said dejectedly.

"As owner of the Cliff House Hotel, I hate for any of my guests to be disappointed. Would you like a free lunch in our dining room?" He reached inside his jacket pocket for one of his cards, on which he was planning to write a note to Raoul, the restaurant manager. But the woman shook her head.

"No, thanks. I have to get back to work." She narrowed her eyes suspiciously. "Why are you being so nice to me?"

She had him there. "Because you're a guest in my hotel."

"It's not as if I have a room or anything. I just came in off the street. I was a guest at the Oilman's Ball, too, but you weren't so polite then."

"You were tossing accusations at me," he reminded her. His collar felt suddenly too tight. He tugged at his tie, loosening it slightly.

"I wasn't doing anything of the sort." Her argument came out a couple of decibels higher. "You jumped to a ridiculous conclusion."

"You said I was responsible for your sister's pregnancy!"

Miranda, the desk clerk, looked over, concern etched in her face. "Is everything all right, sir?"

"Everything's fine, Miranda," he said with a nod and a smile. He returned his attention to the blonde. "You're good at causing scenes, aren't you?"

"I resent that!" she said, her voice yet another notch louder. "If you'd let me finish what I was going to say—"

"Please, Elizabeth." Gossip would soon be flying

through the hotel. Eric Statler had engaged in a noisy, public argument with a woman.

Abruptly she shut up. She was staring at him as if he'd grown an extra ear or something. Then he realized his mistake. He'd called her Elizabeth.

"You!"

"Who?"

"You're...but you can't be!"

"No, of course not."

She brought her face very close to his, so close that with a minimum effort he could have stolen a kiss from those lush, pink lips. "Your eyes are blue!"

"So are yours."

She closed her eyes. "Say something. Say my name."

"I don't know your name."

Her eyes flew open. "It *is* you." Then they narrowed again. "And you were going to leave me swinging in the wind, and soothe your conscience by giving me a free lunch. You took a good look at me and decided I wasn't as attractive as you thought I might be—"

"No, that's not it at all." He supposed there was no use in denying his alter ego now. "Could we continue this discussion in private?"

"In private, where?" she asked suspiciously.

"There's a conference room on the second floor. Believe me, my decision not to reveal myself to you has nothing to do with your looks."

He could tell she wanted to tell him where to stuff his conference room. She wanted to walk out on him. But she was curious; she wanted to hear his explanations. "All right." She picked up her purse and followed him toward the elevators.

They stepped into an empty car, and Eric pushed the button for the second floor. The doors closed. "Elizabeth" hugged a corner and watched him with undisguised interest, arms crossed.

He wasn't going to be able to satisfy this one with any glib explanations, he realized. He was going to have to be honest with her, and hope she understood why he regretted his impulsive phone call to her, and why they should end their association now.

The elevator lurched up a couple of feet, then halted abruptly. Elizabeth grabbed on to the brass hand rail. "Oh, my."

"Oh, no," Eric murmured. He'd made the mistake of getting on the cranky elevator, the one that always stalled.

"Should we push the alarm button?" she asked.

"No," he answered hastily. He didn't want to be found in an elevator with this woman. He could come up with an innocent explanation, but he didn't want to. "It'll start up again in a minute. It always does."

As if listening to him, the elevator jerked into motion again. Eric's sigh of relief was cut short when the car jolted to another stop, and the lights went out.

His companion squeaked a protest, then was quiet. But he could hear her rapid breathing. He remembered she was afraid of the dark.

"They'll fix it in a moment," Eric reassured her. "Whenever there's a problem with an elevator, an alarm automatically goes off in the central engineering room. They jiggle a few switches, and everything works again."

"O-okay," she stuttered, her voice laced with fear.

He couldn't stand it. His mother had raised him to be gallant, to protect those weaker than him. And his father had taught by example. Though considered a chauvinist by some, he never let a lady open her own door or carry a heavy package.

Elizabeth wasn't what he would consider weak, but she was, at the moment, scared, and he had to do something. He reached toward her.

Instead of a vehement protest, she grabbed on to his hand as if it were a lifeline. "I really...really don't like the dark."

"I know." Something happened when their hands touched. He remembered the sensation from the party, but he hadn't realized how strong it was. It was like a closed electrical circuit had been formed. He could feel the waves of energy rolling between them. He could hear it buzzing in his ears.

Instinct took over, and he drew her closer, inhaling her unique perfume. She did not resist or protest.

"It's all right," he soothed. "We're not in any danger."

"No, of course not." She snuggled against his chest, and he buried his fingers in her silky hair. Their mouths found each other, and for a few moments Eric happily drowned in the pleasure of her kiss. The sudden rise of passion was like a third entity between them, coursing through their flesh, binding them, compelling them to join their bodies as closely as possible.

The lights flickered, then blazed brightly as the elevator groaned back to life. Eric knew he should release Elizabeth. Their crazy, magic moment in the dark was over, as was his excuse for holding her, comforting her. But she made no move to let him go, so he held on tighter and kissed her again. What the hell.

The elevator doors opened onto the second floor. Neither of them took a single step toward the beckoning hallway. The doors closed again.

He did not want to talk to this woman in some sterile conference room.

Eric reached for the bank of floor buttons. He pressed the one for the top floor.

"Where are we going?" Elizabeth asked, sounding curious but unconcerned, as if she trusted him completely.

"The penthouse suite is vacant, and I have a passkey."

"Ah." She flashed an impish smile.

"Don't look at me like that. I'm not taking you there to seduce you. I merely thought the suite would be a more comfortable place to talk than some conference room."

"Yes, of course. Can we order room service?"

"No! That is, it wouldn't look good for the hotel's CEO to be entertaining a young lady in a private room. I pride myself on setting a good example for my staff."

As the elevator doors opened on the fifteenth floor, Elizabeth pulled away from him and gave him an amused look. "'Young lady?' What century were you born in?"

He didn't dignify the question with an answer. He couldn't help it that he held himself to a higher standard than most people. As his father, Two, so often reminded him, a long tradition of conservatism and scrupulous behavior went along with the Statler name.

That reputation sometimes was a burden, and Eric could remember secretly envying his half brother, who wasn't saddled with the Statler name. Nick went his own way, beholden to no one. He dated senator's daughters and barmaids. He drank fine scotch or rotgut tequila. He reveled in his outrageousness, if only to tweak Two's nose. And he amassed a small fortune of his own, without the Statlers' help.

Eric, meanwhile, plugged along in the family business, following in his father's footsteps. Sure, he'd taken Statler Enterprises into new areas of industry. The company's net worth had jumped by thirty percent in the four years he'd been making key decisions. But he never took a step, in his professional or personal life, that he didn't first ask himself, "Would Two approve?"

Few understood what a burden it could be, being heir to the Statler empire. There were times—like right now—he wanted to chuck it all for one afternoon of mindless sex with the beautiful, outrageous woman who was charging down the hallway ahead of him as if she knew exactly where she was going.

If it was only his reputation at stake, he wouldn't worry so much. But even the simplest, most basic of indiscretions could have far-reaching, even devastating, consequences.

Chapter Seven

Liz led them unerringly to the door of the suite.

"Been here before?" Eric asked as he first tapped on the door, then opened it with his pass key.

"Uh-huh. On prom night, a group of us rented the suite for a party."

"You were one of the fearsome foursome?"

She gasped. "How do you remember that?" The hotel staff had branded Liz and her friends with that moniker after they'd virtually destroyed the suite with their prom party, which had gotten out of hand when some of the boys had spiked the punch.

"I was working at the hotel that year. I personally scrubbed your wretched punch off the carpeting."

She giggled. "Somehow I can't picture the Statler golden boy on his hands and knees, scrubbing a stain."

"Yeah, well, believe it. My father made me work at the crummiest jobs Statler Enterprises had to offer before he gave me an office. He said he didn't want to just hand it all to me, that I would end up too soft if I never had to work with my hands."

"You think he was right?"

Eric thought for a moment. "Yeah. I was a pretty obnoxious, spoiled rich kid. Just ask my brother. If I'd never had to work as a hotel housekeeper or a hospital orderly, I wouldn't have any concept of what the rank and file go through."

Liz plopped down on the bed, taking in the lush silver carpeting thick enough to get lost in and the brocade draperies. "You've redecorated."

"A couple of times in the past dozen years." He took a chair a safe distance from her, for which Liz was grateful. That kiss in the elevator, unexpected as it was, had shaken her to the core.

She picked at a loose thread on the bedspread. "So…what are we supposed to talk about?"

"I think…" Eric seemed ill at ease, which Liz imagined was out of the ordinary for him. "I think I was going to apologize for standing you up. Or almost."

"It was pretty rotten."

"I never should have called you in the first place."

"Why not? I know you're not married."

He looked uncomfortable. "I'm not…in a position to…date right now."

"Uh-huh." Liz's stomach sank. She was being given the brush-off. "Won't that be a surprise to Valerie Sinclair and Babs Pinkley and, oh, what's that other woman's name—Tiffany Smithersteen."

Eric paled. "How do you know all that about me?"

"I read the society page," she said airily. "You and your debutante girlfriends are mentioned at least once a week."

"They aren't girlfriends. They're escorts. Tiffany's

only twenty-two. Do you really think I would *date* her?''

Liz felt incredible relief to hear him dismiss the glamorous Tiffany so easily. At the same time she didn't like what she was hearing. Not that she had any intention of becoming Eric's girlfriend. Given their rocky recent history, that idea was ludicrous. But she found it sad that anybody would rule out emotional involvements from their lives.

"So you *escort* these women to parties and ballets because…"

"Because it's expected."

"And to keep other women at bay. You must have to beat them off with a stick. You're handsome *and* you're rich, an unbeatable combination."

"You think so?" he asked, lifting one eyebrow. Though he asked the question in a playful tone, she got the distinct impression her answer was more important than he let on. She was his sounding board. How often did he get to talk this frankly with some woman he would never see again—one who couldn't gossip about him because she knew no one influential with whom to gossip?

"I think you would make some woman an upstanding husband," she said diplomatically. "But if you're asking me personally…well, I'm wondering what happened to my pirate. He was a lot more fun."

He narrowed his eyes at her. "Who are you?"

"Elizabeth."

"No really."

"My name is Elizabeth Van Zandt," she insisted. "Most people call me Liz." She flashed him a devilish smile. "But I like the way you say Elizabeth."

He jumped out of his chair and paced. "How do you know my mother?"

"I don't. My sister is painting your brother's portrait." At his look of puzzlement she added, "My sister? The one I mentioned to you who's pregnant?"

"Bridget is your sister?"

"You know her?"

"No. But Nick has...mentioned her."

"Your mother invited her to the party, but Bridget was feeling sick that night and didn't want the costume to go to waste, so I went in her place. I intended to go straight to your mother and introduce myself and extend Bridget's regrets...but then I met this dashing pirate..."

"Is your sister all right now?" Eric asked. It seemed he couldn't think of anything else to say.

"Oh, she's fine. She's just pregnant. I think I mentioned that."

Eric immediately stiffened. "You're not going to bring that up again."

Liz hopped to her feet, ready to do battle. "You never let me finish the story."

"I'm sure your sister's pregnancy is none of my business!"

"Yes, it is! If you would just let me—"

"It's not. Maybe you're mixing me up with my brother. He seems to have a thing for this artist sister of yours."

"You say *artist* the same way you might say *floozy!*"

"I did not. I was merely trying—"

"Oh, I've had enough of this. You may be just about the most handsome man in Oaksboro, Eric

Statler, but you're an insufferable, uptight, judgmental prig.''

She headed for the door.

''Liz, wait.''

She stopped, though she didn't know why. This man had an inexplicable effect on her. But why couldn't they have a normal conversation? Why were they jumping down each other's throats?

A sudden, crazy thought occurred to her. She reached up to the light switch, gritted her teeth and flipped it off. The room plunged into darkness, and her heart leaped into her throat.

''Elizabeth...Liz.'' Eric's voice was ragged. ''I don't think this is a good idea.''

It was a fabulous idea, Liz thought, trying not to hyperventilate, resisting the urge to flip the switch on again. She could get through this. ''Why not? We can't seem to communicate very well looking each other in the eye. Maybe it's because I'm too aware of who you are. And you, unfortunately, are too aware of who I am.'' Which was nobody.

''I'm not a snob, if that's what you're thinking.''

''But you only date girls with pedigrees.'' *What was that?* she wondered frantically. Did something just brush against her? Could the Cliff House possibly have bats?

''I only date women I have no serious interest in,'' he corrected her. His voice sounded closer.

''So there's no chance you'll be tempted to get involved.''

A long pause. ''You have a way of cutting to the chase.'' He was closer still, only two or three feet away.

Liz's heart hammered crazily inside her chest. She wanted to reach out and grab him. If she could just touch him, she would feel so much safer.

Cautiously, she voiced the rest of her theory. "You don't want to see me anymore because…I tempt you?"

"Exactly." He was close enough that she could feel his breath, now. But he still hadn't touched her.

"That's all backward. Why are you so much against getting involved with a woman you're attracted to?"

"Because the woman a man chooses to involve himself with has a profound impact on his life. Even a casual involvement can lead to all sorts of problems, both personal and professional. A man in my position has to be careful not to misstep."

"You say 'in my position' as if being Eric Statler is some sort of holy calling."

"My father seems to think it is," he said dryly.

Liz decided not to go there. "So you bar women completely? Forever?"

He chuckled low in his throat as he placed his hands on her shoulders and drew her to him. "For now. No women. No wives, no girlfriends. Business only." And he kissed her again.

Liz would have laughed at the irony if she hadn't been so moved by his kiss. This man was starving—not for sex, but for intimacy. And somehow, against all odds, he'd found it with her.

She returned his kiss measure for measure. He felt incredibly warm and solid. Somehow, with the dark room and no words between them, she felt closer to him than if she could see his face, with its aristocratic nose and arrogant chin. In his arms like this, he was once again her pirate, plundering for treasure.

Though they ventured into uncharted territory, she was no longer afraid.

"Liz," he murmured against her ear, trying out the shortened version of her name. She liked the way he said that, too. But she couldn't bring herself to say his name in return. She would just as soon forget who he was. This was impossible…impossible….

She slid her hand beneath his jacket, smoothing his starched cotton shirt against the hard planes of his chest. Lord, she thought, he didn't have an ounce of fat on him. Of course, she knew that. She'd seen him almost shirtless the night of the party. She'd plastered her body against him then, too.

"I have…a meeting…to go to," he said between kisses along her neck and collarbone that sent chills rippling throughout her body.

"Then go," she said, even as she let her fingers stray to his shirt buttons. She loosened his tie and undid the first few buttons of his shirt. Skin. She had to feel his skin.

He didn't object. He made no move to stop her, and in fact he held very still as she hesitantly explored his contours. His chest rose and fell in rapid succession.

Somehow, through the sensual haze enveloping her, Liz held on to some semblance of sanity. If he had to be somewhere, it wasn't right of her to hold him here. She was practically seducing him. But if she buttoned up his shirt and let him go to his stupid meeting, would she ever see him again?

She withdrew her hand.

"Don't...stop." He sounded as if forming even those two simple words was a chore.

"I don't want to make you late," she forced herself to say.

In answer, he kissed her again, harder, more insistently. He cupped both her breasts through her silk blouse and thumbed the nipples. She reacted as if he'd touched bare flesh, with a gasp and a moan. Her nipples grew hard inside her bra, and the physical restrictions of her clothing became a burden.

"Your meeting..."

"I'm the boss. What are they going to do, fire me?"

JUST A FEW MORE MINUTES, Eric promised himself. He just wanted to kiss her, hold her, feel her soft, soft breasts for a few more minutes. Then he would end this insane interlude and send the woman on her way. But not yet. Not just yet.

He teased the buttons of her blouse open, needing to feel her breasts unfettered as he had at the party. Would they be as smooth as he remembered? He'd dreamed about those breasts, lush and ripe.

He struggled with the clasp on her bra. The room was utterly dark, and he couldn't see what he was doing, but he wanted it that way. He felt safer. He was afraid that if she could see his face, she would see...what? How he really felt? That she would see what a powerful hold she had on him, sexually?

Not a good idea to let any woman know that, he thought foggily as her jacket, blouse and bra fell away. Aided by her hands, he was pretty sure.

He buried his face against her breasts, pressing them against his cheeks. They were so incredible....

"You're perfect," he murmured.

"Mmm, right."

"I want to make love to you, Liz," he said. Plain and blunt as you please. No pretty words. What was wrong with him? Still, she made no objection. So he swung her up in his arms and carried her to the huge bed.

Everything moved quickly after that. Eric didn't think, didn't consider, didn't evaluate the consequences. He just let his feelings take over. He dispensed with his clothes, tossing them on the floor, not even caring if they got wrinkled. By the time he joined Liz on the bed, she'd managed to lose the rest of her clothes, too. He would have enjoyed undressing her, but was glad for the expediency. He was crazy for her, and he wouldn't be able to hold out for long.

There was no more gentle kissing, no lingering caresses. This was one of those times when urgency took priority over coaxing and murmured endearments. Besides, Liz seemed every bit as anxious as he was. The moment they were together on the bed, she pressed herself against him like a cat starved for affection. Her thigh brushed against his arousal, and he had to bite his tongue to keep from crying out at the unexpected pleasure of even that incidental touch.

"You feel so good," she said as her hands roamed his chest, his back and shoulders, his buttocks, eventually arriving exactly where he wanted them. She was no shy, shrinking violet, and for that he was pleased and grateful. He'd never even imagined a woman whose hunger matched his, much less encountered one.

Liz's did. She kissed as if she meant it, pouring herself into each meeting of their mouths. She threw her long leg over his and crushed her softness against his hardness, and he groaned like a man being tortured. Being tortured to ecstasy.

He worried that she might not be ready, as quickly as their encounter had escalated, but those fears were laid to rest the moment he poised himself to enter her. She was hot and slick and almost pulsating with need. He slid inside her, neatly, snugly sheathed in a custom-made fit.

"Oh, yes!" Her exultant words filled him with male pride.

He echoed them. He couldn't help it. They sounded like a couple of bad actors in an after-hours cable movie, but it just felt so good, so right, that he couldn't hold anything back.

He couldn't recall ever being so uninhibited during sex. No worries about performance, no worries about whether his partner was enjoying herself—clearly Liz was.

Their coupling was relatively short but intense, culminating with a piercing pleasure so sweet it hurt.

Afterward they lay panting in each other's arms, covered with a thin sheen of sweat.

"Well," Liz finally said.

"Well," he said back. What could one say? No words seemed adequate.

Liz leaned up on one elbow and flipped on a bedside lamp. She peered at the digital clock.

"Oh, my God."

"What?"

"Work. I have to get back to work."

Eric didn't want to face reality yet. But with Liz scrambling over him to get to her clothes, he couldn't afford to wallow in fantasy any longer.

Fantasy. Clearly that was what he'd just experienced. And it had no relation to the real world.

"We need more light," Liz announced. "I can't see what I'm doing. I can't find my underwear!"

Taking pity on her, Eric got up and turned on the overhead light. The sudden illumination catapulted Eric back to grim reality. He'd just had sex with a woman he hardly knew. A woman whose motives were a mystery to him.

As he reluctantly rose and rescued his own clothes from a wrinkled pile on the floor, he watched her dress from the corner of his eye. She did not spare him a glance.

Had he come on too strong? he wondered. He'd never, in his whole life, pushed a woman into having sex if she didn't want to. On the other hand, he couldn't remember ever being refused. He was extremely circumspect when it came to lovemaking, and he normally chose his conquests very carefully.

Impetuous, unplanned sex wasn't his style. Until now. But he'd wanted Liz with an intensity totally unfamiliar to him. And he'd done his level best to overwhelm her with his desire. He'd told her in the elevator that he wasn't bringing her to the penthouse suite in order to seduce her, yet that's exactly what he'd done.

"I don't usually do things like this," he said, buttoning his shirt.

"And you think I do?" she said crossly. "Damn, I have a run in my hose."

"Of course I don't think you do," he said. He suddenly felt like he needed to apologize, but he didn't know what for. She hadn't exactly been making a sacrifice to go to bed with him. She'd enjoyed it.

"But you're wondering about my motives now, aren't you?" she asked matter-of-factly. "I could be a fortune hunter, a gold digger."

He laughed. "Listen, Liz. Your look of surprise when you realized I was the pirate was too genuine. Either you're a very good actress, or you like something about me besides my money."

Finally she met his gaze, and she almost smiled. "Yes," was all she said.

Eric felt a comforting glow in the pit of his stomach.

"Can I call you a taxi?"

"I drove."

She was dressed before him. As he struggled to get his tie tied right, she stepped into the bathroom and emerged a couple of minutes later with a powdered nose, fresh lipstick and combed hair.

"Do you want me to go down ahead of you?" she asked.

"No, of course not. I'll walk you to your car."

"It's not necessary."

"I want to." Deciding he was as decently groomed as he was going to get, he opened the door to the suite and allowed her to exit ahead of him. A maid was just emerging from one of the other rooms. She stopped, startled, and stared at Eric.

"Oh, Mr. Statler. What are you... I mean..."

"Surprise inspection," Eric said.

"I was feeling sick," Liz said at exactly the same moment. They both looked at each other guiltily. "Mr. Statler was kind enough to let me lie down until I, um, felt better," she finished lamely.

The maid nodded. "Of course. I'll just...make this room up again."

"Right." Eric pulled a ten-dollar bill from his wallet to tip her. "Thanks. Sorry to inconvenience you."

"It's no trouble, sir." But the speculative gleam in her eye was unmistakable.

Liz said nothing until they were on the elevator—the good one this time, not the one that stalled. "Well, that didn't go so well."

"Don't worry about it," Eric said, but inwardly he was groaning. He was doomed. The desk clerks and housekeeping staff would talk to each other and compare notes. Gossip would spread like chicken pox at a preschool. And his father would hear about it, sooner or later.

Eric could handle Two's disappointment. But he wasn't sure if Two could handle it.

He pressed the lobby button, but the elevator stopped on the second floor. The doors opened, and Dalton Graham stood on the landing. He drew back in surprise.

"Mr. Statler! I...that is..." His nervous gaze darted to Liz, then back again. "I was just coming to look for you. You're always so punctual."

Eric prayed Liz would just smile and keep quiet, but naturally she felt compelled to speak up.

"It was my fault," she said, all in a rush. "I

wasn't feeling well—I was about to faint, really—and Mr. Statler here let me lie down in one of the rooms till I felt strong. He really was quite concerned. You just don't see that kind of concern among strangers—''

"And you are…?" Dalton asked, cutting off her gushing monologue.

"Liz Van Zandt, pleased to make your acquaintance." Liz stepped out of the elevator and extended her hand. Eric followed suit, seeing no other choice. He would have to endure these formalities. "I'm an old friend of Mr. Statler's," Liz finished.

Dalton looked uncertainly at Eric, then back at Liz. "But didn't you just say you were strangers?"

"Oh, well—"

"We haven't seen each other in a long time," Eric supplied, giving Liz a warning look. The explanation didn't even make much sense, but he figured at this point the less said the better. "I'm walking Ms. Van Zandt to her car, and then I'll be at the meeting. Please ask everyone to wait."

Dalton nodded, still looking unconvinced. Eric practically dragged Liz back to the elevator.

To her credit Liz appeared mortified. "I'm so sorry," she said when they were safely away from Dalton. "I never meant to cause you so much trouble."

He surprised her by kissing away the worried furrows on her forehead. How could she apologize for giving herself to him so generously, with so much enthusiasm? "Please don't apologize. If I suffer any consequences, it's my own fault. I'll deal with them."

The elevator doors opened out onto the lobby. Careful not to touch Liz in view of any onlookers, he nonetheless managed to steer her toward the front door.

"Consequences?" she squeaked. She stopped in her tracks, and her face went pale.

"Never mind. You don't have to worry."

She started walking again, but stopped just short of the front door. "You think this was all a big mistake." She looked up at him, her blue eyes gone icy, challenging.

He could hardly deny her accusation. "People get carried away sometimes," he said. "I probably should have shown a little more self-control."

She pushed her hair away from her face, a gesture that made her seem both young and defiant. "That couldn't be more clear." She gave him a smile that came nowhere near to reaching her eyes. "Have a nice day."

He stared after her as she whisked herself out the revolving door. *Have a nice day.* The nicest part of it was definitely over. Now he had to try to repair the damage.

God, he'd been a real bastard, he thought as he hurried back to the meeting room. He'd swindled her into bed, then sent her on her way with a dismissal more rude than he would give an employee he was firing. But it was best that she left angry at him, he decided. He had no business getting caught up with a tempestuous woman like Liz Van Zandt. Without meaning any harm, she could waylay all of the plans he'd been carefully laying out since college.

Chapter Eight

"That's definitely the best portrait you've ever done."

Bridget jumped and dropped her brush at the unexpected voice behind her. She'd been in her studio since dawn, totally engrossed in her portrait of Nick Raines, so the intruder's interruption was doubly alarming.

Fortunately, it was only Liz.

"You might try knocking sometime." Bridget picked up her brush and wiped a daub of burnt sienna from the brick floor. "You really like the picture?"

Liz pulled a chair over and sat down, her gaze still on the portrait. "The guy looks as if he could walk right off the canvas. It looks just like him. He can't help but love it."

Bridget had her doubts about that. It was far from a perfect representation of the complicated man that was Nicholas Raines. Sure, the dark eyes reflected his unique combination of mischief and solemnity, but they seemed too shallow when reduced to two dimensions. The firm, almost arrogant chin was pure

Nick, but the left hand—it looked too soft. Not enough pent-up tension.

"I'm just not sure…" Bridget heard paper rustling, and realized Liz was opening up a paper bakery sack. "What have you got there?"

"Breakfast. I brought one for you, too." Liz pulled a chocolate éclair from the Truelove's bag and placed it on a napkin in her lap, then handed the bag to Bridget.

Bridget's stomach rumbled. It was almost eleven o'clock, and she hadn't yet eaten. She was surprised the baby hadn't given her a sharp kick to remind her. He-she was already proving to be demanding, and Bridget was only in her fifth month.

The morning sickness, thank God, had gone away for good. With a silent apology to her baby for giving it a sugar overload, she grabbed the éclair from the bag and took a huge bite. Heaven.

"So what's the occasion?" She hadn't seen much of Liz the past few weeks, not since their disagreement over her behavior at the Statler party. They'd talked, and Bridget had dutifully forgiven her. She could almost laugh about it now. But Liz had remained a bit distant and distracted. Bridget had backed off, knowing that sometimes her twin needed a bit of solitude to work things out.

"Just wanted to check on you. How long have you been working on this picture, anyway? Seems like forever."

"Way too long." Three times as long as for any other portrait. Sometimes, when she wasn't completely satisfied with a portrait, she would put it away for a while and work on something else. When she returned to the problem picture, she usually would know exactly how to fix it.

Nick's picture defied fixing. She just couldn't be satisfied with it.

"Don't you think it's time to call it quits? You're becoming obsessed with the thing."

Maybe she was. She'd gotten used to the oil-and-canvas Nick being in her studio. She left the painting uncovered, so he greeted her every time she came in here to work. She would miss him. "Mrs. Statler has called a couple of times to check on it, but she's planning on 'unveiling' it at her annual holiday party, so there's no hurry."

"Still, maybe you should—" Liz cut herself off abruptly. Bridget looked over at her. Her face had gone almost gray, and she had a look in her eyes that Bridget knew well. She was going to be sick.

Liz jumped from her chair and ran from the room. Concerned, Bridget followed her, but the bathroom door was closed.

"Liz? You okay?"

Bridget shuddered as she heard the unmistakable sounds of someone losing an éclair.

A few moments later the toilet flushed and the faucet turned on. A few moments more and Liz emerged, face damp, eyes unnaturally bright, and still pale as a ghost.

"Poor thing!" Bridget cooed, empathizing completely. How many times in the past few months had Liz nursed Bridget through a bout of violent nausea? "Come into the guest room and lie down. Do you think the éclair was bad? Or maybe a touch of the flu?" Bridget stepped into the bathroom to get a cold, wet cloth for Liz's head while Liz went on into the bedroom.

"I don't know," Liz said weakly.

When Bridget joined her, she was lying on the bed with an old granny-square afghan drawn up to her chin, a perfect Camille. "I did the same thing yesterday, but then an hour or so later I was better, so I didn't think that much about it."

As she placed the wet cloth on Liz's forehead, Bridget's senses went on alert. "You aren't... I mean, this couldn't be..."

"What?"

"It's just that—"

"Oh, my God."

The twins looked at each other. Liz had figured out easily enough what Bridget was hinting at, and she hadn't immediately ridiculed the idea. That must mean she was seeing someone.

"And you didn't tell me?" Bridget objected, skipping all the dialogue in between. They often spoke in a shorthand that left others in the dust.

"I wanted to, but then it was such a disaster..."

"But it's possible?"

"Yeah, it's possible," Liz admitted, not sounding terribly thrilled. "The weird thing is, when we...you know, I wasn't even thinking about his sperm."

"How romantic that must have been."

"Not really. We were just carried away."

"Then this wasn't a, um—" how could she put it? "—a willing donation?"

"No," Liz said miserably. "But I didn't steal it from him, honestly, Bridge. I swear, I wasn't thinking about that at all. In fact, if I had, I would never have— Oh, God, what am I going to do?'' And she burst into tears.

Bridget sat on the side of the bed and hugged her, unsure what she should say. She had a feeling the tears were about more than a possible pregnancy. When Liz's sobs quieted a few minutes later, Bridget asked gently, ''So who is this fertile paragon?''

''I can't tell you. I won't tell anyone, because I don't want him to know.''

''Oh, Liz.''

''I know what you're going to say. But trust me when I tell you, this guy would not be thrilled about having a baby. In fact, he made it pretty clear he doesn't even want a relationship.''

''Why not?'' Bridget asked, indignant. What man in his right mind would fail to find her sister attractive and desirable?

''It's a long story.''

''Does this have something to do with the billboard?'' Liz had steadfastly refused to discuss the billboard, beyond saying it hadn't produced the desired results.

''No more questions, okay? Besides, maybe I'm worrying for nothing. It could be a touch of the flu.''

Bridget didn't think so. She had a leftover home pregnancy test in the bathroom cabinet, and she'd dig it out later, when Liz was feeling better. But for right now, the poor thing probably just wanted to be left alone. Bridget covered Liz up with the afghan, told her to take a nap, turned out the light and slipped out.

Bridget had other problems besides a miserable, morning-sick sister in her guest room. Nick was coming over in exactly forty-five minutes. That was the real reason she was so jumpy this morning. In all of their sittings she'd never given him even a glimpse of the painting, but sooner or later she had to. Today was the day.

If he ridiculed it or derided her painting skills in any way, she would just curl up and die. She would. She'd worked harder on this darn painting than anything else in her entire life. She wasn't sure why it was so important. Of course, she wanted the Statler family to be pleased with her work. They had lots of wealthy friends who might be in the market for portraits, and a few referrals from them could give her career a real boost. But that wasn't the only reason she'd stayed up late nights worrying about Nick's portrait.

If he liked it, she would call it quits, she decided. She would sign her name to it, crate it up and send it to Geraldine Statler. Then she would focus her time and attention on her other commissions. Honestly, her business had been suffering a bit due to her obsession. Her mother's cousin had hired her to paint her granddaughter. The kid would be in college before Bridget got around to it, at the rate she was going.

The doorbell rang at quarter to twelve. Bridget's stomach swooped. Why was she so nervous? She was ready for him. The house was immaculate, and she was looking as good as a woman her size and shape could look, having taken extra care with her grooming this morning. Liz was snoozing soundly, and Bridget had decided to just let her sleep it off.

Wiping her damp palms on her skirt, she headed for the front door.

AS HE HEARD feminine footsteps click-clicking toward the front door, Nick suddenly wished he'd brought Bridget some flowers. Or at least a cup of gourmet decaf coffee from Truelove's. They'd parted on such poor terms last time he'd seen her, almost a month ago. He'd kicked himself a dozen times a day since then for carrying on that ill-fated morning about her sleeping habits. *What* had he been thinking?

He'd been a sick, jealous wreck, that was all.

The door opened, and Nick's breath caught in his throat. She was a vision in a soft-looking, black wool dress that draped gently over her growing stomach. Her blond hair was pulled back in a sedate ponytail at the nape of her neck, held with a black velvet ribbon. She wore minimal makeup, if any, and her feet were encased in black patent-leather granny boots.

Her face looked too pale, though. Was she ill? Or had she just lost all of her summer tan?

"Good morning, Nick," she said with an uncertain smile. "Come on in out of the cold."

"Morning. You look great." The words just slipped out.

"I look fat," she corrected him. "But thanks."

Fat was not the word he would have chosen. *Burgeoning*, maybe. *Lush. Madonna-like*. He'd never realized pregnant women could be this attractive.

"Would you like something to drink?" she asked, the perfect hostess, as she took his bomber jacket and hung it in her hall closet as if she was afraid it would wrinkle.

"Coffee?" he asked hopefully.

She shook her head. "These days I can't stand the taste of it, or even the smell. Herbal tea?" she countered.

"Never mind, I'm not *that* thirsty. So, let's see this masterpiece."

"It's not a masterpiece," she said emphatically. "I'll warn you right now, I'm not happy with it. Maybe you'll be able to figure out what's wrong with it. We still have a couple of weeks before your mother's party."

"I'm sure it's fine," he soothed. She seemed awfully nervous about this. Truthfully, he didn't care that much about the portrait. So long as he was marginally recognizable, he would be happy. Then again, given how angry he'd made Bridget, he wouldn't be all that surprised if she'd gotten her revenge by making him look like Quasimodo.

"You just don't want to pose for me again," she argued.

Nonsense. He'd missed her this past month. Even Dinah missed her, in a way. Nick had fallen into the habit of coming to work every Wednesday morning and reporting to his receptionist how his portrait sitting had gone. He would gripe and complain in an overblown fashion, doing melodramatic imitations of himself and Bridget until Dinah laughed so hard she fell off her new office chair. It had become a ritual.

"If you need me to, I will," he said, as if it would be a supreme sacrifice.

"I hope that won't be necessary."

"Was I really such a drag?" he asked.

She paused at the entrance to a small solarium, which he could see had been transformed into a painting studio. "Of course not. I always enjoy my sessions with a live model."

"But I thought this live model in particular got your dander up."

"From time to time," she conceded with a slight grin. She resumed walking, leading him into the studio.

The small but airy space was bright with winter sunshine, though some of the blinds were drawn to keep direct sunlight off the canvases in various stages of completion. In addition to several portraits, Nick spotted a landscape, a still life, and a couple of modern, nonrepresentational pieces.

He paused in the middle of the room, looking around him. "You are really good."

She blushed prettily. "Thank you."

"No, I mean it. Are all these commissions, or are they for sale?" He was drawn, in particular, to a still life of a grouping of wine bottles, some empty, some half full, along with a corkscrew and some wineglasses containing liquids of various hues. The scene looked so real it made him thirsty.

"That one I'm doing for my own amusement. I work Saturdays at a co-op gallery downtown, and sometimes I show my work there."

"I want this one," he said impulsively.

"It's not finished," she objected. "And you don't even know what the price is."

"Doesn't matter. I'll buy it."

She narrowed her eyes suspiciously. "Are you trying to butter me up for something?"

"Why would I do that?" Why indeed? he wondered. He really did like the picture, but he wasn't an art connoisseur. He'd never bought a painting in his life. Was his gesture merely a transparent effort to get back into her good graces?

"Guilt," she answered succinctly.

"If you don't want to sell me the picture, just say so."

She studied him for a moment, as if trying to peel back his skull and read what was in his head. Then she looked back at the picture. "I'll let you know when it's finished, and we can talk about it," she finally said. And then, sounding as if she was forcing the words out, "I appreciate your interest."

Finally Nick's gaze was drawn to the one canvas that was covered up. It stood on an easel in the center of the room, a sheet draped over it.

Bridget went over to it and grabbed the sheet, then paused. "Trumpet fanfare?"

Nick obliged with an off-key "Ta-*dah!*"

Bridget whisked off the cover, and Nick suddenly found he couldn't breathe. Now he knew how Bridget and her sister felt when they looked at each other. The man in the oil portrait was him, down to the last minute detail.

"You hate it," she said glumly.

"No, no. I'm just awestruck, that's all." He stepped closer, then leaned in until his face was inches from the oil-on-canvas Nick's face. "I've seen lots of pictures of myself, but nothing has ever come close to this. It's like looking in a mirror. A slightly flattering one,'' he added.

"Flattering, my aunt Fanny. I don't know how to tell you this, Nick, but yours is not a face that can be easily reduced to two dimensions. I don't think I came even close."

"Am I hearing right? Are you actually paying me a compliment?"

"Why wouldn't I?"

"Because you think I'm the devil incarnate?"

"Even a devil can be handsome." She turned her gaze away, finding a piece of lint to pick off her sleeve.

Nick was inordinately pleased she found him attractive. He'd never lacked for female company. Women had always seemed to like him, even before he had money. But few had ever gone out of their way to tell him they liked the way he looked. Having been compared to Eric the golden boy most of his life, he'd never thought of himself as particularly handsome.

The way Bridget was looking at him now, he felt handsome. Like the best-looking guy in the whole town.

"Are there, uh, any changes you think should be made?" she asked. Then she cleared her throat and looked away.

"I always wanted green eyes."

Instead of laughing, she looked almost stricken.

"No, just kidding. Really. The painting is perfect. My mother will go into a rapture when she sees it."

"You're sure?"

"Yes. Damn, Bridget, stop selling yourself short.

How do you ever make a living at this if you're so insecure about your work?''

"Not all of my work," she huffed. "Just this picture."

"I guess I'm flattered. And I'm sorry I was so difficult. You're not even making any money on this painting."

"It's good PR." She covered the painting back up. "I'll arrange for delivery tomorrow."

"Okay." Was that his cue to leave? *Just turn toward the door. Walk out of here and don't look back.* He had no business feeling what he was feeling for a woman carrying some other man's child. "Could I at least take you out to lunch?"

"That's nice of you, but my sister is asleep in the guest room. She's not feeling well, and I don't want to leave her alone."

"Nothing serious, I hope."

"Just a flu bug. Or something." A look flashed across Bridget's face, amusement or consternation or something else Nick couldn't identify. Then it was gone.

What was that all about?

"Speaking of your sister, I've been meaning to ask you. Did she have anything to do with that billboard out on—"

"Oh, please. Let's not go there."

"Then it *was* her."

"It was a big waste of money."

"Then the, um, pirate didn't respond?"

"No, he—" Bridget halted, a thoughtful expression on her face. "She never said that exactly, now that I think about it. She said it didn't work out. But

I wonder…" She counted something silently on her fingers. Then she gasped. "Oh, my God. That's it." She grabbed Nick's arm. "Liz said she was dancing with some pirate at your mother's party. Do you happen to know who that might be?"

"I already told you. My brother, Eric. But she denied it and you wouldn't believe me—"

"Not your brother. A guy with long, dark, curly hair, a full beard, and brown eyes."

Nick laughed and nodded. "Yeah, my brother. He was wearing a helluva costume. Some friend of his who works in the costume department of a movie studio did a number on him. Brown contact lenses and everything. Eric walked within two feet of my mother and she didn't have a clue it was him."

Bridget's eyes had grown larger with every word Nick spoke. "Oh, my God."

"What?"

Then she suddenly got nervous. "Nothing, nothing." She forced a smile. "Sorry you have to rush off."

"I do?"

"You don't want to hang around here."

"Why, because I might catch Liz's flu bug?"

"Oh, I don't think there's much chance of that."

Nick could tell he was being gotten rid of. Apparently, whatever magnetic force drew him to Bridget wasn't as strong on her part. Though he knew it would be best for all concerned if he just got out of there and forgot he ever knew Bridget Van Zandt, her rejection hurt.

But could he blame her? After some of the stupid things he'd said to her? Why would any woman want to hang around some judgmental jerk who'd come out and told her he thought she was selfish and wrong for having a child out of marriage?

She led the way briskly out of the studio, through the living room and toward the hall closet, where she'd hung his jacket. Man, she wanted him gone. And he could think of nothing, absolutely nothing, to prolong his stay or his acquaintance with the most intriguing, beautiful woman he'd ever met. There were depths to Bridget he hadn't even begun to plumb.

Then fate stepped in. Not in a way Nick would have chosen, but it worked. In her haste to reach the closet, Bridget caught her foot on the edge of an Oriental rug.

It happened in slow motion. Nick saw her start to pitch toward the coffee table. Suddenly all he could think about was that she was pregnant, and that coffee table was nothing but sharp edges. He made a flying leap worthy of a Super Bowl wide receiver diving for a pass in the end zone.

He didn't exactly catch her, but he did break her fall. *He* was the one who took the brunt of the coffee table, which collapsed noisily as he fell on it. He heard something else shattering, too, like pottery or glass. Bridget landed half on top of him, half on the floor.

In the unearthly silence that followed the crash, Bridget didn't say a thing. She lay there, one hand curled protectively over her stomach as she gasped for breath.

"Don't move," he cautioned, easing his arm out from underneath her. Though his own back was in

an agony of pain, he ignored it. "I'll call an ambu-
lance."

She grabbed his arm and shook her head.
"I...just—" she struggled to get each word out
"—got the breath...knocked...out of me."

"You might really be hurt," he persisted.

"So...might you." She was struggling to breathe,
but she was managing to suck some air in, then out.

"Yeah, but I'm not pregnant. Please. Let me at
least take you to the hospital to be checked out. If
anything happened to your baby..." He was surprised to hear his own words choked with emotion.

"Why would you care? You don't think I should
be having it in the first place."

"Don't even think that," he said fiercely. "I may
disagree a little bit with your methodology, but I
know how important this baby is to you and would
never want anything to happen to him or her."

Bridget closed her eyes. "I'm sorry. I shouldn't
have said that." She was breathing more easily now.

"No, you shouldn't have. But I guess I never
should have said how I felt about it to begin with. It
was none of my business." He struggled to sit up.
Every muscle in his back protested, but he didn't
think anything was broken besides the table.

Bridget started to sit up, too, but he placed a hand
on her shoulder and held her down. "Not yet. Can
you move your feet?"

She sighed. "Yes, I can move my feet. Nothing
hurts, not my neck, not my head. I just knocked the
wind out of myself. Now let me— Oh!"

"What?" All sorts of terrible possibilities flew into

Nick's mind. Spinal injury, punctured lung, miscarriage—

"Just the baby kicking. I guess he doesn't like the rough treatment." She sat up then and scooted around so she was leaning against the sofa. "Oh, there he goes again. Gracious, he's really mad."

"Is it a he?"

"I don't know. My doctor doesn't believe in sonograms without a definite reason to have one. Ow!" Then she giggled.

"I'm calling my doctor." He started to get up, but she pulled him back down beside her.

"No, silly. I'm fine." Then she grabbed his hand and placed it on the swell of her abdomen. He started to protest and pull away. This was far too intimate a contact, especially for someone who'd done nothing but scoff at her pregnancy. But then he felt a definite jab against the palm of his hand, and he knew a sense of wonder he hadn't felt since he was a kid.

"There's really a baby in there."

"Did you think I'd made it up?"

"I guess babies don't seem very real to a guy till they're out in the world, screaming and needing their diapers changed."

"What a lovely view of parenthood you must have."

He shrugged. "Just what friends have told me." He hadn't removed his hand. When the baby kicked him again, he chuckled. He realized he could have sat there all day, inhaling Bridget's perfume and feeling her baby beneath the firm mound of her pregnancy.

She looked up at him, her big blue eyes luminous,

and something indescribable passed between them. He felt a surge of protectiveness and covetousness so strong it nearly knocked the breath out of him. When their lips touched, it seemed kissing was the perfect thing for holding on to the moment.

He'd imagined kissing Bridget, of course. What red-blooded man wouldn't within ten minutes of meeting her? But his imagination had been a feeble substitute. Her lips were so soft, like baby skin. He put his arms around her, angling her body closer to his. He inhaled her distinctive fragrance as he plunged his tongue into her mouth, overcome with a need to possess her.

Bridget, far from passive, wound her arms around his neck and passionately returned the kiss. She seemed as hungry for him as he was for her.

A door opened somewhere else in the house, dimly registering on Nick's consciousness.

"Bridget?" a concerned voice called out. "What was that terrible crash?"

Sanity returned with the drama of a bucket of cold water. Nick reluctantly released Bridget, and they both pulled apart like guilty teenagers caught making out in the back seat. But not soon enough.

Liz, hair mussed and clothes rumpled, stood at the entrance to the living room, mouth hanging open. "You okay?" she finally asked.

Bridget put her face in her hands. "Never better," she mumbled.

Liz took in the coffee-table-turned-kindling and the shattered remains of a china something that had once graced the table, then turned a megawatt smile on Nick. "Man, that must have been some kiss!"

Chapter Nine

Bridget knew she should thank her sister for interrupting the passionate moment between her and Nick. It was completely inappropriate for her to be lying on the living room rug playing dueling tongues with a client. But instead, she wished she had a sling shot.

Nick, at a definite loss for words, had started to push himself off the floor, but Liz stopped him. "Don't get up on my account. I was just leaving."

"Are you feeling well enough to drive?" Nick asked, seeming genuinely concerned.

"I'm much better, now. Ta, Bridget, call me later."

Liz whisked past them to the front door, which opened, then closed behind her with amazing speed.

Bridget groaned. "I'm sorry, Nick."

"Sorry? Because you have a sister with a smart mouth?"

"For throwing myself at you," she admitted. "I've been feeling lonely lately, wishing I had somebody close to share everything with. I mean, you were the first person besides me to feel the baby kick. And I just went crazy there for a minute."

"Stop apologizing. It was a nice kiss, okay? We're not going to hell just because we gave in to a perfectly natural urge between two adults."

"If I wanted to thank you for breaking my fall, maybe a batch of cupcakes would have been more appropriate."

He slid an arm around her. "I hope there was more than gratitude involved."

Oh, boy, was there. The rush of longing that had enveloped her when Nick was feeling her baby kick was one of the strongest biological urges she'd ever felt. She'd imagined, for just one crazy moment, that they were a couple, that he was the father of her baby, sharing a normal joy most married couples shared.

But the moment had been counterfeit, manufactured. She had given up all those normal, happy moments when she'd decided to be artificially inseminated. She'd thought the joys of motherhood alone would be enough.

She'd been wrong.

Not that she would change what she'd done. She wanted the baby inside her more than anything in the world, even the love and companionship of a good man. But she hadn't realized how much she would miss that special man in her life.

Unable to resist, she rested her head on Nick's shoulder, allowing herself to steal just a few more moments of this warm companionship. "There was more than gratitude involved," she assured him.

They were quiet for a long time, but Bridget could almost hear Nick thinking. *What do I do now?* He'd gotten himself into quite a bind, making a play for the pregnant lady. She knew he didn't want to hurt her feelings—deep down she suspected he was a pretty decent guy, even if sometimes he spoke before he thought. She was going to have to help him out.

She took a deep breath. "I don't expect anything, you know."

"Excuse me?"

"This was just one of those weird things that happen. I'm not expecting any follow-through. You'd be crazy to want to start anything with a woman in my position."

"Nobody ever said I was sane."

Bridget's heart beat a little faster. What exactly was he saying here?

"I'm incredibly attracted to you, Bridget. I have been since the moment I laid eyes on you."

"I find that a little difficult to believe, given that I look like I swallowed a melon."

He laughed softly. "I can't explain it, either. I'm just calling it how I see it."

She sighed. "I'm drawn to you, too. Shoot, that's an understatement. You're darn near irresistible. But I'm not really in a position to…"

"To what?"

"To start anything. I have this baby to think about. I don't want you to think I'm daddy shopping."

"That never occurred to me. I'm hardly daddy material."

She pulled away to look at him. "Why would you say something like that?" If she *were* daddy shopping, she wouldn't immediately scratch Nick Raines off her list. Despite his harsh condemnation of her decision to become a single mother, he'd always shown her care and consideration. The way he'd risked life and limb to break her fall was a perfect example. He treated his mother well; his employee, Dinah, thought he walked on water, so he obviously was fair to her.

Why wouldn't he make a good father?

He didn't meet her gaze. "You've read the stories about me, I'm sure. I'm the black-sheep brother. The wanderer. I never stick with anything very long, including women."

It was a pat answer, and one that didn't satisfy her in the least. "I don't put much stock in newspaper gossip. Anyway, you don't stick with any one thing very long because that's the career path you've chosen. You build up a business, sell it and move on. I suspect that once a business is on firm footing and operating smoothly, it's not a challenge to you anymore."

"And how do you explain about the women?"

"Hmm. You must like the challenge of a new conquest." Sobering thought. Was that why he was attracted to her? She represented a bigger-than-average challenge?

"You see?" he said gently. "You aren't exactly describing a man to whom home and hearth are a number-one priority."

She thought about his tidy white frame house with its blooming flower beds and the green, healthy houseplants and the warm skylights. He was a nester if ever she'd seen one. But since he was trying to make a graceful escape from her life with all his excuses, she decided to let him.

"You're right," she said briskly, moving all the

way out of his light embrace. "This is an academic discussion, anyway. I decided from the beginning I was doing this parenting thing alone. I don't want a series of 'uncles' or stepdads for this kid. The only way to ensure stability for him or her is to not get involved with men in the first place. So it's a moot point." She smiled as if she was completely happy with her decision. But she wasn't. She hadn't realized, until about five minutes ago, how great a sacrifice she was making.

He stood up, wincing as he did.

"Oh, Nick, are you okay?" Focusing so strongly on the baby's welfare, she hadn't seriously wondered whether *he* might be injured.

He smiled. "Nothing a soak in my hot tub won't fix." He reached down to give her a hand. She rose slowly, testing her weight, but nothing seemed out of whack.

"I'm not even sore," she said, amazed. "But my poor coffee table. Not to mention my grandmother's teapot."

"I'll help you—"

"No, really, that's not necessary. I have somewhere I need to be, so it'd be best if you left. I'll get Liz or my mom to help me with this mess later."

It was a fib. She had no appointments this afternoon. But she needed him gone. That broad chest of his, those strong arms, were just too tempting.

"All right, then. If you're sure?"

She nodded.

He got his jacket from the closet. "You really did a great job on the portrait. It was worth every penny I spent and more."

"Thank you. I'll take that to heart."

She kept the smile plastered on her face as he walked out the door. She listened to the sound of his truck engine starting, then receding. Then she very deliberately walked back to the couch, sat down and had a good cry. She was long overdue.

STEPDAD. That was one role Nick Raines was determined never to play, he thought as he drove down Bridget's street and out of her neighborhood. He was glad Bridget had reminded him of that.

When Geraldine Raines had married, Two had accepted his new wife's child into his home, but never into his heart. He'd provided financially for Nick, but he'd never shown him the slightest bit of paternal affection. When Geraldine had tentatively mentioned the possibility of her new husband adopting Nick, Two had told her in no uncertain terms that it would never happen. He was a very wealthy man, and no one other than a flesh-and-blood son would inherit his fortune.

His mother and stepfather hadn't realized he'd been eavesdropping.

In Bridget's living room just then, he'd been entertaining some dangerous fantasies. For a split second he'd seen himself in a husbandly, fatherly role. But what kind of father could he be? He certainly hadn't had any glowing examples in his life to follow. He'd never even met his biological father. The swine had taken off before Nick was ever born. He didn't know the first thing about raising children, and he didn't want to know.

He liked his life just fine. He went where he

wanted to, when he wanted to. No one to answer to. Just now he'd made a narrow escape from a dangerous sand pit, and he was lucky Bridget's thinking was similar to his. She'd let him off easy.

But for some reason he didn't feel so damn lucky.

ERIC'S SECRETARY, Sandra, wordlessly handed him another pink message slip as he came back from lunch. Middle-aged, maternal Sandra was the soul of discretion. He didn't have to worry about her gossiping to co-workers about a series of mysterious phone calls from someone named Liz, phone calls he apparently wasn't returning, given the fact that she kept calling back.

He'd meant to call her back. He wanted to. He intended to. But he never could seem to find the right time.

He knew what he had to do. But if he talked to her, if he heard her sexy voice, it would call to mind all those crazy, wonderful moments they'd shared, and he would have a really difficult time actively dismissing her from his life.

It wasn't that he didn't want to see her again. *Want* was a pale word to describe the craving he felt for her company, her body, her soul. He wanted to be with her again with an intensity that was driving him crazy. But the timing was so incredibly wrong.

Two was finally going to retire, something he should have done five years ago, given his health. He'd suffered two mild heart attacks already, and his doctor had told him in no uncertain terms that he needed rest and relaxation. The stress of running a multimillion-dollar conglomerate was going to kill him.

But it was only in the past few months that Two had felt confident enough in Eric's leadership to actually hand over the reins. The lawyers were drawing up the paperwork now. A meeting was scheduled in one week's time. Then an official signing ceremony, a restrained retirement party, and it was done.

For most of his life, Eric had made his father proud. The only time Two had been disappointed was during that business in college. Coincidentally, that was also when Two's first heart attack had occurred.

Since then Eric had devoted himself to being the son his parents could depend on. He was good as his word, solid, never mentioned in a gossip column except in glowing terms—unlike his black-sheep brother, who had managed to make a success of himself despite cutting a wide swathe through Texas. Even his mother, who was far easier to please than Two, had urged Eric to do whatever was necessary to earn his father's confidence, so that Two could retire as soon as possible.

If Eric suddenly appeared with an outrageous woman like Liz on his arm, a woman who made him do crazy things, his mother would faint from shock, his business associates would start doubting his judgment, and his father would yank the reins away so fast Eric's head would spin. And then, under the stress of running the ever-growing corporation, the old man's heart really would give out.

Eric had to keep an even keel, at least for now.

He headed for his office. He would call Liz back

right now. She must have a reason for calling him so persistently.

He would be firm. He would tell her he could not, at this delicate point in time, waver from his single-minded devotion to running Statler Enterprises. Not if he wanted his father to live to a ripe old age.

He opened his office door, intending to head straight for the phone. But there was just one problem. Two was sitting behind his desk.

"Ah, there you are," the older man said. He stood up, leaning heavily on his cane, and Eric was struck anew by how age was really catching up with his father. In a few short years he'd gone from a robust, distinguished executive to a florid, dissipated shadow of his former self. "Took kind of a long lunch, didn't you?"

Ah, hell. He was thirty years old, and his father was still keeping track of his lunch hour. Eric didn't honor the criticism with a defense; it was pointless, anyway. "What's up, Dad?"

"I snuck past your girl out there. Didn't want anybody to know I was here."

"Why not?" Since Two apparently had no intention of relinquishing his position behind Eric's desk, Eric sat down in one of the wing chairs facing him.

"Because this is a private meeting. I don't want anyone to even know it's happening."

The hair on the back of Eric's neck stood at attention.

"Mum's the word. What's going on?" *Please,* he prayed, *no disasters that would convince Two he had to stay on.*

"You're taking over the reins of Statler Enterprises in a week's time. Giving over the power to you wasn't a decision I took lightly."

"I know that."

"A few of the vice presidents aren't that happy about such a young man having so much responsibility."

"I know that, too." He'd talked personally with each vice president, most of them closer to his father's age than his. He'd convinced each of them that, as a young man with infinite energy and ambition, an intimate knowledge of every facet of the corporation and a reputation to protect, he was the perfect candidate to run things, and all had grudgingly agreed to at least give him a chance.

"I've been hearing rumors I'm not too pleased about."

Uh-oh. This could only be one thing.

"Please tell me you weren't entertaining a blond floozy in the Cliff House VIP suite."

And that's an order, Eric added bitterly. But a heated defense of his behavior wasn't what Two wanted. Eric kept his facial expression pleasant, his voice low and relaxed. "First off, she wasn't a floozy. She's the sister of one of Mother's friends." The truth, strictly speaking.

Two's bushy eyebrows rose in question. He wanted more.

"She's an ad executive who'd gone to a great deal of trouble to meet with me." Also true. "I offered her a short meeting and a tour of the facilities. She had some very interesting notions, actually." Eric smiled, remembering exactly what some of those notions had felt like.

"And that's it?"

"If you heard more...well, you know how small things get inflated once the gossip mill gets hold of them."

Two seemed to relax. "Good, then. A man with poor moral judgment often shows poor business judgment, as well. I couldn't in good conscience turn over my company, the company I built from nothing, to a man who can't manage his personal life with compunction and dignity."

"No, of course not. Dad, aren't you supposed to be at home resting now?" Something like this could really set his father back. He didn't look quite healthy—his face was too red for one thing.

"Damn doctors. I can't rest at home when the future of my company is in question."

"The company is fine, Dad."

"And it's going to stay that way!" On that note, Two left the office with little fanfare, apparently no longer concerned that Sandra or anyone else would see him leaving, now that the potential crisis had been avoided.

As soon as he was alone, Eric sat down, more shaken than he'd like to admit. He hadn't technically lied to his father, but he certainly hadn't told the truth. The feeling made him uneasy.

He looked at the pink message slip, still clutched in one sweaty hand. He couldn't call her now.

Carefully he placed the message slip in his desk drawer, under some papers, hoping he would at some point be struck with inspiration as to what to say to Liz.

Hell of a life he'd built. Successful, dependable—

and sterile as a hypodermic needle. But at least it was keeping his father alive.

SOMEONE POUNDED insistently on the front door of Liz's apartment. She cracked one eye open and peeked at her clock radio. Ten-thirty. Ah, hell, she'd slept through her alarm clock again.

"Hold on, I'm coming," she grumbled as she threw herself out of bed. The nausea hit immediately, but she was getting used to it. She grabbed a robe from the back of her bathroom door, but she took her time putting it on, half hoping her morning caller would give up and go away. Probably the paperboy, or her neighbor, who more than once had accused Liz of stealing her newspaper.

Liz peered through the peephole. Bridget, looking perky and carrying a thermos bottle.

Liz sighed. She supposed there was no use trying to duck her sister anymore. Bridget had called half a dozen times in the past three days. Liz could only put her off for so long.

She opened the door.

"Liz. Are you okay? I was worried about you. I called you at work, and they didn't know—"

"I'm fine, I'm fine. Just overslept." She let Bridget in, then plodded toward the kitchen, still half-asleep. Coffee. She needed caffeine. "Want some coffee?"

"Liz! You can't drink caffeine if you're pregnant."

Liz paused in her reach for the coffee carafe. "Really?"

"Are you pregnant?" Bridget asked.

Liz supposed there was no ducking this question, either. Pregnancy was notoriously hard to hide. Or it would be in a few months. "Yeah," she said with a smile she couldn't quite contain. "I got a bun in the oven."

Bridget hugged her. "Oh, Sister, I'm so happy for you. We'll raise them together. They'll only be a few months apart in age. Won't that be fun? It's how we always dreamed it would be."

"Yeah, except those schoolgirl fantasies we spun usually involved husbands, too."

Bridget released Liz and looked her in the eye. "Obviously I blew that. But is there no chance for you?"

Liz plopped down in a chair at her kitchen table. "He won't even return my calls."

Bridget's jaw dropped. "That son of a—" She reconsidered what she was about to say. "Here, I brought herbal tea. It's good for you." She busied herself getting cups from the cabinet.

"It's not that I want to marry him or anything," Liz said hastily. "He made it abundantly clear he didn't want a relationship. Which played right into my hands, right? I wanted a donor, I got one."

"But?"

"But I thought he ought to know. About the kid."

"Maybe not," Bridget said as she poured out the steamy, peculiar-colored tea, reversing her earlier opinion. "If the guy's such a Neanderthal he can't return phone calls, maybe he doesn't deserve to know."

It seemed to Liz that Bridget was watching her too carefully. Like she was trying to get a rise out of her.

"He's not a Neanderthal," Liz said quietly. "It's just that he has a wall of protection around him like Fort Knox. I don't have his home phone number, because it's unlisted, so I have to call him at the office. And he's got this bulldog of a secretary. Maybe she's not passing on my messages. I don't know."

Bridget's eyes twinkled with mischief. "I bet I can get to him."

"You don't even know him." Liz took a tentative sip of the tea. "Yuck, what is this stuff?"

"Chamomile. Add a little honey if you don't like the taste. It's great for morning sickness. Trust me. And I know his brother."

Liz nearly spit out her second sip of the vile tea. "What are you talking about?" But her indignant question didn't come close to fooling Bridget, who simply gave her a knowing smile. "How did you know it was Eric?"

"Nick mentioned his brother's pirate costume. It wasn't that hard to put two and two together."

"Then you know what a pickle I'm in. You *do* remember Eric's and my first conversation, right? I was just trying to make light conversation, and he accused me of wanting to sue him for paternity. Can you imagine what his reaction will be when I tell him I'm for-real pregnant? He'll go ballistic!"

Bridget actually shuddered. "Maybe you shouldn't tell him," she said again.

"I have to. You're the one who told me it's not ethical to steal a man's sperm. What's the worst that can happen? He'll yell and scream and claim it's not his, I'll say okay, and I can go on my merry way."

She took another sip of the tea. The taste was growing on her, and her stomach did feel calmer.

"If it's what you really want."

"Then you can help?"

"Give me a couple of weeks. I think I can arrange a meeting. And he won't even know what's hit him until you've got him in a headlock."

Chapter Ten

It was New Year's Eve, and Bridget felt like a hippopotamus. She would just as soon have spent the last two months of her pregnancy hibernating in her own little house. And she would, she promised herself. Just as soon as she got this party over with.

It wouldn't be polite to skip Geraldine Statler's holiday gala, not when she was the guest of honor—and not when she'd played hooky from the last party Geraldine had invited her to, causing an embarrassing incident, to boot.

She could hardly believe Geraldine had been kind enough to extend an invitation to Liz after Liz tried to steal her fan. But when Bridget had mentioned how much she wanted to spend New Year's Eve with her twin sister, Geraldine hadn't hesitated in sending Liz an invitation. Nick's mother was a truly warm-hearted lady.

So here she was, driving up to the Statler mansion in a limo, no less—Geraldine had insisted. Bridget had asked Liz to ride in the limo, too, but Liz was running late and said she'd meet Bridget there.

A valet rushed to open the limo's back door.

Bridget climbed ponderously out of the car, already regretting her choice of dress. But formal maternity gowns were hard to come by. This one's alternating panels of yellow and black velvet made it elegant and distinctive, and would have made a dazzling statement on someone with a waist. Instead, it made her look like a bumblebee. She couldn't imagine what prompted her to buy it.

Geraldine and Two were hanging out right by the front door, greeting guests as they arrived. Geraldine didn't hesitate to put her arms around Bridget.

"Oh, my dear, don't you look a vision," she said. "Some women really know how to carry a pregnancy with class. The coat check girl is right behind you if you'd like to leave your wrap."

"I don't feel so classy," Bridget admitted, removing her black faux-fur jacket.

"Oh, don't be silly. Two, doesn't she look a vision?"

The distinguished-looking older man extended his hand. "Don't believe we've had the pleasure."

"Two, this is our portrait artist, Bridget Van Zandt."

Bridget shook his hand. "Pleased to meet you."

He murmured a greeting, then turned to another guest. Bridget couldn't shake the feeling that he faintly disapproved of her. Then again, a man of his generation probably would disapprove of any pregnant woman seemingly flaunting her condition.

"The band should be starting up in the ballroom, Bridget dear, and there's all manner of food in the dining room."

"Thank you, Geraldine," Bridget said warmly.

She handed off her jacket to the waiting clerk, then she plunged into the party, already well into swing. She spotted Mrs. Hampton and chatted a few minutes with her, then went off in search of a cold soda.

She found one in the kitchen. Usually that was where she liked to hang out at a party, but the professional catering staff obviously had things under control there. She wandered around some more, trying valiantly to make small talk, but she was so bad at mingling, especially when all she wanted was to get off her feet.

She finally found some much-needed solitude in the music conservatory. The room was pretentious, hung with gilt-framed oil paintings and two monster chandeliers, but it was quiet, and Bridget couldn't resist the lure of an ebony grand piano.

She'd never seen such a fabulous instrument in her life. She sat down on the bench, opened the lid, and caressed the ivory keys. She tried out a couple of scales, enough to know the piano was in perfect tune. Before long she was deeply engrossed in her favorite Chopin sonata.

She was dimly aware of the sound of a door opening and closing, but she didn't stop playing. Surely no one would object to her playing the piano, and since there were bowls of nuts and garlands all over the room, she didn't figure it was off-limits to the guests.

Then someone sat down on the edge of the bench next to her, close but not close enough to hamper her playing. She knew without even looking who was there. He said nothing, so she finished the piece.

When the last notes faded away, Nick applauded.

"Very nice. I didn't know you played in addition to being an artist."

"Seven years of lessons. I'm rusty, though."

"Sounded fine to me."

She turned to look at him. God, he was handsome in what looked like a new blue suit. His tie, when she looked closer, had little reindeer all over it. "Nice tie," she said with a chuckle.

"Don't you start, too. My mother was all over me. She's the only women who can get me into a suit at all, you know."

Personally, Bridget would like to be the woman who got him out of his suit.

With a mental slap of her own wrist, she pushed all the lascivious thoughts from her mind and focused on her goal for the evening—getting Eric and Liz together. "Well, you look handsome."

"And you look beautiful. And healthy. No ill aftereffects from the fall?"

"None at all. You?"

"Back surgery. No, just kidding," he said when she started to gasp. "A bruise the size of Texas, but that's all."

She punched him playfully on his arm. "Don't scare me like that. Oh, Nick, I..." She couldn't quite get the words out.

"What?"

"I miss you, that's all."

"I meant to call," he said, looking away.

"I could have called you, too. Look, just because we can't get involved doesn't mean we can't still be friends, does it?"

"A man and a woman can't be just friends. Didn't you see *When Harry Met Sally*?"

She didn't know whether he was teasing her or not. She decided he must be. Of course they could be friends. "Ridiculous. We're friends, whether you like it or not. And in your official capacity as my friend, I need a favor."

"Uh-oh."

"It's not that bad. I just need your help playing matchmaker."

A wary look came into Nick's velvety gray eyes. "Who's the lucky couple?"

"My sister. And your brother."

"Liz and Eric?" Nick burst out laughing.

"Oh, come on, it's not that funny. You know they were playing kissy face at your mother's masquerade party."

Nick seemed thoughtful. "That was really out of character for Eric, I must admit."

"They saw each other once after that."

"Really?"

"But now he won't return her phone calls."

Nick stood up and spread his hands in a helpless gesture. "Love is fickle. What can I say?"

"But they really need to talk. Face-to-face. She's coming to this party, and I already spotted Eric. We just have to get them somewhere together, alone, and let nature take its course."

Nick was already backing away from her. "No. No way. I've never interfered with my brother's social life, and I'm not starting now. Besides..."

"What?"

"I can't see any future in it. Really."

"Why not?" Bridget demanded. "Isn't Liz good enough—"

"No, it's not that. It's just that Eric is...well, he's married to Statler Enterprises. He just officially took over the reins, you know."

"No, I didn't know."

"He works night and day. Mother had to threaten him with all sorts of dire things just to get him to this party. He wanted to work New Year's Eve, can you imagine?"

"Then he needs someone like Liz. To lighten him up."

Nick shook his head. "Truth is, I wouldn't do that to Liz. When Eric marries, it'll be to some social-climbing debutante who can entertain herself with shopping and tennis and volunteer work, and who won't expect an emotional commitment from him."

"That's horrible."

"Not a life I would choose for my sister, if I had one."

Bridget sighed. If what Nick said was true, that explained why Eric hadn't called Liz. Still, the man had to be told. "Nick, I have to tell you something. In confidence."

"Okay."

"Liz is pregnant."

Nick stared incredulously. "You Van Zandt sisters don't have a whole lot of sense when it comes to reproduction, do you? Are you trying to create your own private population explosion, or what?"

That did it. Bridget pushed herself up from the piano bench with a noisy screech. "Let me tell you something, you insensitive clod! Liz and I didn't make single motherhood our first choice. But in case you haven't noticed, neither one of us has men lined up to marry us. And it isn't that we haven't looked. But neither of us has ever found anyone we could love and raise children with and grow old with. It's all you men wanting to protect your precious independence and your devotion to your blasted careers that drive women like Liz and me to take more creative measures.'' She barely paused to take a breath. "So just back off with the criticism!''

"You're right, I shouldn't have—''

"You could try thinking once in a while before you spew out your ill-thought-out judgments. And anyway, Liz didn't mean to get pregnant. It was an accident.''

"So why do you want to get her together with Eric? Not only does Eric not want a girlfriend, he can't abide scandal. Two would go ballistic if his golden boy took up with a pregnant woman.''

"Well, maybe Eric should have thought of that before he knocked up my sister!''

Nick appeared genuinely stunned. "Are you...are you saying Eric is... Uh-uh. No way.''

"Of course he's the father.''

"But Eric would never do that. He's...well, you just don't know him. He's the most careful, painstaking...he plans and plots out every step he takes, right down to his choice of tie or where he eats lunch. He would never...''

"Shows how much you know!'' Bridget snapped.

He didn't quite know how to respond to Bridget's angry retort. So he stood there just staring. Then the music room door opened and Two himself walked in, breaking the tension.

"Bridget, were you playing that piano?" he asked genially.

"Um, yes." Should she apologize?

But Two's smile put her at ease. "Geraldine plays, too. I bought her that piano for a twenty-fifth anniversary present."

"It's lovely." Bridget stroked the ebony wood, thinking how nice it would be to have a husband that generous and considerate after twenty-five years.

"Anyway, Geraldine meant to tell you she plans to unveil the portrait at ten o'clock. So don't wander too far away." He cast a sideways look at Nick, almost a warning, Bridget thought. What was that all about?

"I'll be around." She observed with interest the way Two and Nick watched each other, like a couple of wary wolves vying for territory.

"The picture's wonderful, by the way," Two said. "You really captured Nick's arrogance."

Nick's eyes narrowed. Bridget murmured a thankyou, appalled that Mr. Statler would compliment her and insult his stepson simultaneously.

Two turned toward Nick. "I've been thinking, Nick, maybe we should put that painting in a place with better light than the library. Like in here, for instance."

Bridget tried not to wince. She couldn't imagine her very masculine portrait mixing very well with the gilt and crystal of this feminine-looking room.

Nick said nothing.

"Well, I'll talk to your mother. She'll put it where

she wants, I imagine." With that, the older man left, thumping his cane on the parquet floor with each labored step.

"That son of a bitch," Nick muttered.

"I'm sure he didn't mean that like it sounded," Bridget said, her own anger toward Nick dulling as she picked up the urge to defend him. "A crusty old businessman like him, he probably thinks arrogance is a good quality. And he did say he wanted to display the painting in a room with good light."

"You think that was meant as a compliment?"

"Well..."

"Come with me." He took her arm and all but dragged her out of the conservatory and down a long hallway, to a part of the house that was obviously for family use only. They passed a cozy TV room, and then entered a dimly lit, foreboding library. The room reeked with the smell of lemon oil, old leather and mildew, along with the wood smoke scent from a small blaze in the natural stone fireplace. Along one wall were floor-to-ceiling bookshelves overflowing with ancient-looking tomes that probably no one had bothered to read in a hundred years. On the opposite wall was a long line of oil portraits in carved mahogany frames—every Statler male from the last four generations, Bridget guessed.

The last portrait in the line depicted a boyish-looking Eric Statler III, painted in this very library. Bridget studied the portrait of Nick's half brother— the father of Liz's baby—with her artist's critical eye. It was a good painting, she admitted. But that somber expression on the subject's face bothered her. He looked as if he was worrying far too much for a young, prosperous man in his twenties.

Finally she saw what Nick wanted her to see, a blank space on the wall next to Eric's picture. That space was where his mother intended Bridget's painting of Nick to be hung. And his stepfather, with his hearty suggestion for hanging the portrait in the conservatory, had made his feelings abundantly clear: he didn't want Nick's picture included with the Statler men.

"Oh, Nick..." She didn't know what to say.

"You don't have to feel sorry for me. I don't have any burning desire to join up with the Statler dynasty. I just wanted you to understand..." He didn't finish the thought, but gazed out the window into the winter darkness, lost in a world of hurt that he couldn't quite hide with a glib comment. No wonder he'd reacted the way he did to her decision to have a baby without a father. His expressive eyes reflected the remnants of a little boy deserted by his real father, who craved acceptance and affection from a surrogate. And who never got it.

She couldn't help herself. She touched his arm, then his hand. He wouldn't have appreciated any sort of sappy platitude, so she just said what she was thinking. "Eric Two is a gold-plated turkey."

Nick smiled, a little sadly, and squeezed her hand. "Yeah. And I hate like hell what the old man is doing to my brother."

"Eric? I thought Two was turning the whole company over to him."

"With a million strings attached."

"Oh." It hadn't occurred to her that Eric might have a few troubles of his own to deal with.

"Eric has spent his whole life trying to measure up to one yardstick or another. Two adores him, but that love had to be earned. Earned and earned again, constantly. Eric learned early on that any failure, any deviation from the very narrow path Two laid out for him met with severe penalties."

"That must have been a tough way to grow up."

Nick shrugged. "Fortunately, Eric usually found it pretty easy to meet and exceed expectations. He's always known the right thing to do—in business, sports, social situations. He turned out a pretty good guy, despite the pressure Two put on him. But he doesn't know how to relax and let go—never has."

"Which is why you find it so hard to believe he might have fathered a child out of wedlock?"

"Exactly."

"But, Nick, every man has a breaking point. Nobody can be a saint 24-7. And some things are just out of a person's control."

Bridget could have sworn Nick's eyes blazed a bit brighter at her reminder. Or maybe they simply reflected the orange flames from the fireplace. At any rate, the look he gave her made her own internal fires burn hotter.

"Like what you do to me." Nick still had hold of her hand, and he drew her closer, pulling her arm behind him and encircling her in a light embrace.

Bridget started hyperventilating even as her own arms, seemingly without her will, stole around his hard body, snugging it up against her. They shouldn't be doing this. She knew it, and he knew it, but she didn't know how to put a stop to it. When he bent his head to kiss her, she met his mouth eagerly with hers.

He kissed her long and hard, the fingers of one hand buried in her hair, the other hand grasping her bottom and pulling her closer still. She couldn't imagine why her stomach wasn't getting in the way, but somehow they fitted together nicely.

When he pulled away, breathing hard, she half expected him to thrust her from him. The expression on his face told her this wasn't in his game plan. But the passion flaring between them wasn't something easily dismissed.

"I can see," he said on a ragged breath, "how Eric might've gotten swept away. Liz is a very attractive woman."

The compliment was meant for Bridget. Her face felt suddenly warm. "And Liz has a figure."

"You have a figure, too." Nick brought one hand around to caress the mound of her pregnancy. He did it with reverence and maybe even a little awe. He gazed back at her, looking puzzled. "I don't know why I find it so appealing, but I do."

For a few seconds, anyway, Bridget stopped feeling like a hippopotamus. She felt beautiful, basking in the sun of Nick's admiration.

"Come upstairs with me," he said, barely whispering the words.

"Your mother's waiting for me."

"Not till ten o'clock. Any other objections?"

She tried to formulate all the sensible, practical reasons they should not give in to their passions. But not one of them made it past her lips.

Before she knew it, the zipper at the back of her dress was sliding down.

"Not here!" she objected.

He pulled away from her and headed for the door. Her stomach did a panicky flip-flop. Had she driven him off with her caution? Then he flipped a lock on the library door and turned off the lights, leaving the library bathed in the dull orange glow of the dying fire.

She sighed with relief. It was hard to believe how much she wanted Nick Raines. Maybe it was just her insecurity about her increasingly shapeless body, but it mattered a lot to her that Nick found her attractive.

When he returned to her side, he offered her his arm and led her over to a sofa with buttery-soft leather upholstery. Before he allowed her to sit down, he reached for the dress and started to pull it over her shoulders.

He paused, looking pensive. "It's okay for you to do this, isn't it? We won't hurt the baby?"

His concern melted away any lingering reservations she might have had. "My doctor said no dangerous sports. No horseback riding or rock climbing or cliff diving. He didn't say a thing about making love."

With a devilish smile, he pulled the velvet dress off her shoulders, then off her arms, then down, where it pooled around her feet. "Mmm, even better than I imagined," he said, his gaze focusing on her breasts, thank goodness. The pregnancy had made her breasts plumper than usual, so that she'd had to buy all new bras. This one was pink and lacy, and Nick tested the texture of the lace with one finger, sending shivers coursing through her like shock waves.

She moaned, and her knees gave out. He caught her and eased her down on the sofa. "Are you always so responsive?" he asked as he shrugged out of his jacket and kicked off his shoes.

"I dunno," she managed, watching with interest as one article of his clothing after another hit the floor. After studying him for all those hours during the portrait sittings, she'd vividly imagined what he would look like without clothes. She'd come close, but her fantasy wasn't quite as good as the real thing.

She wanted to devour him.

If she'd had her old slim figure back, she would have enjoyed peeling off layers, teasing him. As it was, she just got rid of her clothing as quickly and efficiently as possible, then urged him to lie down beside her on the huge old couch. She preferred him looking into her eyes.

"You don't have to be embarrassed," he said, stroking her stomach. "You're absolutely beautiful."

"You have to say that. You're seducing me. If you compared me to, say, a walrus—"

"Stop it."

"—I'd be out of here in a flash."

He silenced her self-recriminations with a kiss, and then she really did forget about everything except how good it felt to be flesh to flesh with Nick, how good his hands felt everywhere they touched her. And he did touch her everywhere. He knelt on the floor next to the sofa and kissed her, too, in places she'd never been kissed—inside her elbow, on her ribs, on her sensitive instep.

"Nick!" she finally objected when he started sucking one of her toes. "What are you doing?"

"A very thorough job of loving you, I hope."

"My feet are ticklish!" But she wasn't laughing.

When he'd had his thorough, wicked way with her, and she'd perpetrated a few wicked tricks of her own, he lay down beside her and pulled her on top of him as if she weighed no more than a cat.

"Comfortable?"

"Never better."

"I don't want to squash your, um, cantaloupe."

"He's a junior watermelon by now. And you won't squash him. He or she is protected pretty well." With that she straddled his hips and brought him slowly inside her, letting her body gradually accommodate itself to him.

As they established a lazy rhythm, he gazed directly at her, never breaking eye contact even when their movements grew more urgent, more frantic. She had this incredible feeling that he never lost sight of exactly with whom he was making love, which for some reason made her heart swell until she thought it would burst right through her chest.

She reached her crest of pleasure just seconds before he did, trying to hold on as long as possible to the beautiful moment of ecstasy. She'd never imagined sex could be so…spiritual, she thought, for lack of a better word. It was more than a simple satisfaction of a physical urge. But she didn't know how to describe it, or if she even wanted to. Just by looking into his eyes, she knew he understood.

She lay next to him, silent, for several minutes, and was surprised when tears spilled from her eyes.

Why, oh why, couldn't she have met Nick Raines *before* she'd gone to that sperm bank? How different things would be if Nick had fathered her baby!

But he hadn't, and she'd best not forget that.

Chapter Eleven

Liz arrived at the Statler party at nine forty-five. She turned her Miata keys over to the valet, held her head high and walked through the grand front doors of the Statler mansion.

She had second thoughts about her dress. Was it too showy? She did have a bona fide invitation this time, but she still felt unusually awkward.

The house was bulging with party guests, some of them looking as if they'd indulged a bit too freely in the champagne. Liz received a few admiring glances from men young and old, but she was in no mood to engage in a flirtation. She was here for one purpose only: to corner Eric Statler III and tell him the facts of life.

She would make it clear from the very beginning that she wanted nothing from him that he did not want to give freely. That should put his fears to rest. Maybe then he could look at the situation objectively. Maybe then he would sweep her into his arms, kiss her and tell her how much he wanted her to be the mother of his firstborn…and maybe a famous movie producer would ask her to be in his next film.

Liz didn't see Eric anywhere in the throng. For that matter, she didn't spot a single soul she knew, and she felt the urge to fade into the background. Funny, she'd never been shy. For the first time she had an inkling of why Bridget wasn't fond of parties.

She checked out the buffet, but nothing there tempted her. Small wonder. She'd been nauseated all day and had barely pulled herself together in time even to make this late entrance.

She turned away from the food and almost ran smack into her sister—dressed in the exact same yellow-and-black dress Liz wore. Even their hair was styled the same, though Bridget's was slightly mussed.

They stared at each other, speechless for several seconds. Then Liz burst out laughing. "I can't believe we did this again!"

"Fortunately, no one can get us mixed up," Bridget said, patting her stomach. "They'll just think we dressed alike on purpose."

Liz didn't care what anybody thought—except for Eric. "Is he here?"

Bridget knew exactly who "he" was. "I saw him earlier. If you'd arrive anywhere on time—"

"I was barfing, okay? Surely you remember—"

"Yes, yes. Sorry." She gave Liz a sympathetic pat on the arm. "Oh, look, there's Eric."

Sure enough, the man she'd been thinking about nonstop for the past few weeks was standing near the stuffed mushrooms, talking with a very attractive redhead.

Bridget gave Liz a little shove. "Go get him."

"But he's—"

"It's never stopped you before."

Bridget was right. She'd never let anybody stand in the way when she wanted something. She had to give it her best shot. "All right. Wish me luck."

Liz lost sight of Eric as she worked her way through the throng, and when she reached the mushrooms, he was gone. Looking around in a panic, she spotted him heading out of the room, the redhead on his arm.

Damn. What if he was taking her upstairs to…no, no, it didn't bear thinking about. She took off after him.

Eric escorted his lady friend down a hall and through a set of French doors. Not a bedroom, Liz thought with supreme relief. When she reached the doors, she peeked through them and watched for a minute or so. Eric and the woman appeared to be simply talking, nothing more. Working up her courage, she pushed the door open and waltzed inside.

The other two occupants turned to look at her. The redhead smiled pleasantly. Eric looked like a deer caught in headlights.

"I hope I'm not interrupting," Liz said breezily. "The crowd in there is just so thick. I needed some fresh air. What a beautiful room!"

Eric finally found his voice. "Liz. I didn't realize you'd be here."

"I'm not crashing again, if that's what you're thinking. I have a real invitation this time."

Obviously sensing the tension, the redhead started to look uncomfortable. "We can talk later, Eric," she said, heading for the door. "Just give me a call."

He nodded, and she left Eric and Liz alone.

"Sorry if I broke up your little tête-à-tête," Liz said, not at all sorry.

"That was my cousin Julie. She was hitting me up for a job." At least Eric had the good grace to look guilty. "I was going to call you. As soon as I figured out what I wanted to say."

"Meanwhile you left me feeling pretty foolish," she said, settling down on one end of the piano bench. If she didn't sit, she was going to fall. But she'd rather be nudged with a cattle prod than admit to Eric how thoroughly he unnerved her—and how very much this conversation meant to her.

"I'm sorry," he said. "Things at work—"

"That's a crummy excuse, and it's beneath you." She didn't mean to antagonize him, but she couldn't help it. As usual she had to speak her mind. "Your ignoring me, as if I wasn't even worth acknowledgment, was worse than an out-and-out rejection. I would think your mother raised you better."

"She did. I never meant to leave you hanging indefinitely." He sat down on the bench next to her. "I needed to figure out in my own head what I wanted, before I talked to you and really messed things up."

She softened. Maybe he was tossing her a well-rehearsed line, but she didn't think so. "And have you? Figured out what you want, that is."

"Yes, I think so." He didn't look so sure, but she would at least listen to what he had to say.

"And...?"

"I already told you I'm not in a position to start a serious relationship. I don't know if you read the business pages, but I just officially took over as CEO of Statler Enterprises.''

"Congratulations," she said without a lot of sincerity. As a matter of fact, she devoured any section of the newspaper that was likely to mention Eric's name. She knew about his new position. She also knew he'd already been running the corporation for a while, so she wasn't inclined to let him use the new title as an excuse.

"A lot of people are watching me, waiting for me to fall on my face. My personal life isn't my own right now."

"Uh-huh." He was killing all of her far-flung hopes, one by one.

"Relationships take time and attention. If I had a woman in my life, I would want to make her a priority. And I can't right now. It wouldn't be fair."

"Lots of busy people have relationships, Eric. Do you envision a time when you won't be so busy?"

He didn't meet her gaze.

"Your father married and raised you, and he's been running Statler Enterprises for thirty years. Don't you deserve the same chance? Not that I want to marry you," she hastened to add.

"Funny you should mention him." A shadow crossed Eric's face. "His health isn't good."

"I'm sorry." What, she wondered, did that have to do with anything?

He proceeded to tell her. "Though he cares for his family, his heart and soul really belong to that company. He sacrificed a lot to it, including his health. His doctor said if he didn't relax, he was going to die. Period."

"His heart?" Liz asked.

Eric nodded. "Mom persuaded him to step down as CEO and let me take over. But one misstep on my part, and he'd be back working sixty-hour weeks. That's why I can't afford to be distracted right now. Maybe someday..." He trailed off, as if even he didn't really believe what he was saying.

"I'm not asking you to marry me," she reiterated. "I just think everyone deserves a personal life."

"I'm expected to marry at some point," he said. "My father even went so far as to give me a list of candidates."

"Ah, I see. Somehow, I'm guessing my name isn't at the top of the list. Or the bottom. Or the middle."

"Look, I don't take that list seriously. I can marry whoever I want. I just told you that so you'd realize what people expect of me."

"I don't care what people *expect* of you, Eric. I want to know what you want. If you want me to go away and leave you alone, I will. But just tell me. Stop with the stupid excuses."

"I don't want you to go away, damn it."

"Then what?"

He wouldn't look at her. "Have an affair with me."

His words turned her heart into a piece of cold lead. Well, she'd asked for it. She wanted honesty, and by God, he'd given it to her.

"An affair," she repeated. The word had such a nasty connotation. She thought of affairs as what married people did behind their spouses' backs. "In secret, you mean."

"A discreet relationship," he corrected her. "I

could…buy you a house. A nice one, where we'd have all the privacy we want. I couldn't promise you a lot of time together right now—"

"But I could just sit at home in this hypothetical house and wait for the leftover scraps of your life you choose to throw my way, is that it?" Liz was appalled, insulted and outraged. She wanted to slap him, but she managed to control the urge.

"We could spend time together and get to know each other without the pressure of the outside world bearing down on us," he continued.

"Because this 'outside world' you refer to wouldn't approve of me."

"You don't understand—"

"I understand way too well. And what would happen if you got your oh-so-inappropriate mistress pregnant?"

He blinked a couple of times at her, obviously thrown off by her question. "We would take precautions, of course."

"It's too late for that, I'm afraid." It wasn't how she intended to break the news. But there it was.

He stared at her, comprehending the situation all too well. "I'll be damned," he said softly, almost to himself. "I should have seen it coming." He skewered her with a stare that no doubt left many a business rival quaking in his boots. "How much do you want?"

"What?" Surely he wasn't suggesting…

"That's what this is about, right? You think I'm going to pay you a million or so in child support?"

She couldn't believe her ears. "You listen to me, you arrogant jerk. I want nothing from you. I'll go to my lawyer first thing Monday morning, and I'll have papers drawn up absolving you from all responsibility.''

Eric's face turned to stone. Without a word he stood and walked out of the conservatory, back straight as a fire poker.

THE PORTRAIT UNVEILING went off without a lot of fanfare, much to Nick's relief. He and Geraldine stood on one side of the picture, Bridget on the other, while Geraldine gave a brief introduction about how the portrait was purchased and how thorough and exacting the artist was. Then she pulled off the cover to a round of applause. Even Two clapped, though he never stopped scowling.

Conspicuously absent were Eric and Liz. It didn't bother Nick that his brother had chosen to duck out. Nick himself would have skipped the pomp and circumstance if his mother hadn't insisted on his presence. But he wasn't even sure Liz had made it to the party. He hoped Bridget's feelings weren't hurt.

Bridget, who obviously wasn't accustomed to being in the limelight, smiled at all the attention and turned a pretty shade of pink. When Geraldine urged her to say a few words, she murmured something about what a challenging subject Nick had been and how she hoped she'd done him justice.

And that was it.

A couple of people came up to talk to her about doing their portraits, so Nick stayed out of the way and let her sell her services. When he realized she was going to be occupied for some time, he wandered off to find a beer.

He felt a little strange about what had happened in the library. He'd wanted it, he'd pushed for it and he'd reveled in the act of making love. Bridget was an energetic and generous lover, a lot less shy and reserved than he'd guessed she would be, and the whole experience had left him speechless.

But afterward Bridget's silence worried him. Maybe if he'd offered her some reassurances that this wasn't some casual fling for him, that he truly cared for her. But the right words hadn't come, and he surely didn't want to use the wrong ones. He couldn't, in all honesty, offer her anything long-term, nor did he believe that was what she wanted.

He'd toyed with the idea of making Bridget a permanent fixture in his life. But it wouldn't be fair to even ask that of her, not when she'd made it clear she didn't want a man in her life. Especially not a man who was so clearly bad father material.

After a few minutes he went looking for her. Maybe he didn't know what to say, but the least he could do was be there for her. He was her friend, sex or no sex, and that wasn't going to change.

He couldn't find her anywhere. He fervently hoped she hadn't cut out, now that her presence was no longer required.

He peeked into the conservatory, and there she was, at the piano, idly fingering the keys. He watched her from behind for a few moments, his heart aching to say and do the right thing. He didn't want to hurt her.

She poised her fingers on the keyboard as if to begin a piece. He expected to hear Chopin or Beethoven or Brahms. What he heard was "Chopstix."

A few measures, anyway, before she hit a bad note, then an angry, discordant bunch of keys, then silence. Her shoulders shook.

Oh, God. Had he done this to her?

He strode toward her, determined to set things right. Then she turned and he immediately realized he'd made a mistake. This wasn't Bridget, it was Liz. He would have known even if he hadn't noticed the missing junior watermelon.

Liz quickly wiped her eyes. "Oh, hi, Nick, um, I was just—"

"What's wrong?" Maybe it was that she looked so much like Bridget, but he felt strongly protective toward her.

"Nothing." She thrust her chin forward and pasted on a smile. He gave her a look that told her he wasn't fooled for a minute, and her smile faded. "Well, nothing you need to worry about."

"My idiot brother made you cry," Nick concluded. "Want me to beat him up?"

She managed a quick laugh and a hiccup. "How did you know that?"

"Bridget told me."

Liz's eyebrows arched up in disbelief. "How... how much did she tell you?"

"Everything," he said gently.

"Blabbermouth," Liz muttered.

"Don't be mad at her. She was only trying to help you. She thought I might intervene with Eric on your behalf once I knew what really was going on."

A new harshness stole over Liz's features. "Yeah, well, don't bother. Eric thinks this must be a sinister plot to get money out of him."

"He said that?"

"That was *after* he asked if he could set me up as his mistress. Classy, huh?"

"I'll kill him."

"Would you?" she asked sweetly. "I thought about doing it myself, but I don't want my child to be born in jail."

Nick was glad she could maintain a sense of humor, but beneath her flippancy was a pain that ran miles deep. "What in God's name was Eric thinking?" Nick asked no one in particular. "That he was too perfect to father a child out of wedlock? That if a mistake was made, it couldn't have been his? Throwing blame around isn't something Eric normally does," he ended almost wistfully.

"Maybe it was my fault," Liz said glumly. "I didn't get pregnant on purpose, but…well, after all, subconsciously I did want a baby."

"That doesn't absolve Eric of responsibility."

"Look, Nick. I don't need a white knight. If Eric doesn't want a part in this kid's life, no problem. The last thing my child needs is a father who resents him."

That made Nick think of Two. "Eric would never resent his own flesh and blood. Give him a chance, Liz. He'll come around." If Nick had to kick his butt from here to Hawaii first.

Liz shrugged. "I'm not sure I want him to. Once certain words are spoken, it's hard to take them back."

Which was exactly why Nick was having such a hard time saying anything to Bridget. If he blew it now, he might not get another chance. "Have you seen Bridget?"

"Not lately. But if I know Bridget, she's either hiding out in the kitchen trading recipes with the catering staff, or she's found a quiet corner and a good book."

"If you find her, tell her I want to see her before she leaves."

Liz eyed him speculatively, then flashed him a mischievous smile. No sign of her earlier tears remained. "I'm sure she'll be interested to know that."

ERIC WAS ON HIS THIRD SCOTCH, hoping the liquor might put his cockeyed world right side up. But the view was still crooked as hell.

He was hiding out in the library, where he didn't have to smile and be cordial to friends and business associates. He was much more comfortable here, sitting on the old leather sofa, communing with long-dead authors and a fire that had burned down to embers.

The heavy wooden door creaked open. "Go away," Eric called out, realizing he sounded half-lit. "This is a private party."

Whoever the interloper was, he strode boldly into the room ignoring Eric's warning. Eric felt a moment of unease. His parents were lax about security during a party, and there was more than one person on the guest list who wished Eric would disappear. Then the man's form took shape, and Eric sighed with relief.

"Oh, it's you. Thought it might be an assassin or something." Eric started to take another sip of his drink when the glass was jerked rudely out of his hand. He looked up into the decidedly peeved features of his half brother.

"You're going to wish an assassin had found you before me," Nick ground out.

Uh-oh. Eric stood up to be on equal footing with Nick. He was an inch taller than his older brother, and he kept his body in excellent physical condition with daily workouts at Statler Enterprises' private health club, but Nick had always been the better fighter.

Not that Eric and Nick had ever seriously tangled. Still, something gleaming in Nick's eyes worried Eric. He tried for a casual tone. "What's got your hackles up?"

"Didn't our mother teach you better?"

"What are you—"

Nick grabbed Eric's jacket lapels and backed him up against a bookcase. "You made her cry, Eric. You degraded her, you insulted her, you made terrible accusations—"

"She was crying? Liz?"

"Like her heart was broken."

"Can you blame me for being suspicious? After what Kelly Townsend—"

"That was a different situation entirely. You never slept with Kelly Townsend. She was out to ruin you from the get-go."

"And how do you know Liz isn't out to ruin me?"

"Because she's a nice person."

"Nice? You should have heard some of the things she said to me."

"Really?" Nick smiled and slowly released Eric's lapels. "Good for her."

Stepping away from the bookcase, Eric straightened his jacket and rolled his shoulders. "I guess I had it coming."

"She should have closed the piano lid on your head."

"You're enjoying this aren't you. All these years you've been waiting for me to fall on my face."

Nick was suddenly serious, intensely so. "You're wrong there, Eric. I've been waiting for you to turn into a human being. Humans aren't meant to be perfect. We make mistakes. And if we're highly evolved enough, we own up to them."

Eric slumped, all the fight gone out of him. "When I finally screw up, I do it royally."

"Getting a girl pregnant was an honest mistake. But treating her like dirt afterward—that's a screwup."

Eric's jaw clenched. "She doesn't want me in her life. She said she would sign papers absolving me of all responsibility."

"Is that what you want?"

"I don't— No, of course not." He ran his fingers through his hair, though it never did anything except fall perfectly back into place. "It's my kid, too. This thing just came out of left field. I wasn't prepared." He studied his older brother. Once he'd thought Nick had all the answers. Then he'd grown up and thought he held all the answers himself. Now he wondered whether Nick might know a thing or two about human nature that had been neglected in Eric's education. "I don't get it. Why doesn't she want anything from me?"

Nick shook his head. "She wants lots of things

from you, Eric. But she only wants what you'll freely give. I don't know how you missed it, oh brainless one, but Liz Van Zandt is smitten with you.''

AFTER TWENTY MINUTES of increasingly frantic searching, Liz found Bridget in an out-of-the-way powder room, hugging the toilet. Her face was the color of pea soup.

Liz went down on her knees beside her sister. ''Bridget, what's wrong?''

''What does it look like?''

''You can't still be having morning sickness at seven months!''

''Relax, it's not that. I just…I don't know. The stress got to me, I guess. I was queasy to begin with, so I didn't eat anything, and then Geraldine made me talk to all those people.'' Bridget leaned back on her heels and put her face in her hands.

Liz put a consoling hand on her shoulder. ''Poor Bridge. I was getting worried about you. Should we call your doctor?''

''No, I have these little upsets all the time. It's nothing.''

''Okay, if you're sure. Oh, Nick's looking for you.''

Bridget peeked at Liz through her fingers. ''He is?''

''He said you weren't to leave without seeing him first.''

''Oh, no.'' Bridget grabbed on to the edge of the vanity and pulled herself to her feet. Then she looked at herself in the mirror. ''Oh, *no*, he can't see me like this.''

Liz had to concede that Bridget looked a fright. Aside from her sickly complexion, her mascara was smeared and her hair had come loose from the tortoiseshell combs, identical to Liz's, that had held it in place earlier.

She turned to Liz with a panicked look in her eye. "I'm too sick to face him. You have to sneak me out of here."

"Do you know how hard it is to sneak a two-hundred-pound bumblebee *anywhere*? Besides, Nick'll be way disappointed if he misses you. I think you've made a conquest."

Liz was blatantly fishing, but Bridget didn't bite. "I'll call him later. Please, can we just leave while I'm feeling well enough to walk? And I only weigh 140, thank you very much."

They managed to wend their way through a couple of back hallways and into the kitchen, which thankfully had a door to the outside. Moments later they were at the front of the house, where Bridget's limo was parked. "Oh, darn," Bridget said, "I forgot my jacket."

"Want me to go get it?" Liz asked.

Bridget shook her head. "I'll get it another time. I just want to get home to my own bed. Come on, I'll give you a ride home."

Liz climbed in eagerly. She would worry about her car later. "So, what's with you and Nick?" Liz asked, determined not to let her sister wiggle out of this one.

The light in the limo was dim, of course, but Liz could have sworn Bridget blushed. At least she didn't look so green anymore.

"Nothing," Bridget replied, flashing a sad smile.

"Nothing my foot. I'll bet you kissed him again."

Bridget could evade, Liz figured, but she couldn't out-and-out lie, not to her twin. Liz would know in an instant.

"We might've kissed," Bridget said.

"And…?"

"None of your business."

"You did it with him!"

"Would you stop it? We're not in junior high. Anyway, whatever happened, it can't lead to anything."

"Why not?"

"I planned to do this child-rearing thing on my own, remember?"

"That was before any good men showed up. You can always change your plans."

"He might be a good man, but he doesn't want to be saddled with another man's child. He made that abundantly clear."

"Must run in the family," Liz groused.

"Oh, don't tell me…not Eric, too?"

"He's got his damn company. I hope it keeps him warm at night."

Bridge sighed. "Well, what the hell. We've got each other, right? And the babies. Who needs some lousy, irresponsible man, anyway?"

They nodded their agreement in unison. Then they each sank into the limo's plush interior, lost in private thoughts.

Chapter Twelve

Bridget awoke the next morning none the worse for her illness the night before. She wolfed down a huge breakfast of homemade waffles, then did what she'd been promising herself for a long time: she went to work on the nursery.

Her spare bedroom was already painted a lovely pale-yellow. She'd moved the existing furniture to the attic. Then she'd bought a huge, round, hooked rug with ducks on it, and her mother had sent over her old whitewashed-pine crib, dresser and rocking chair. She'd bought a new changing table and a wicker bassinet for the baby's first few weeks.

But there was still lots to be done, and her project for today was a duckling wallpaper border along the wall next to the ceiling. The directions on the package sounded simple enough.

Anything to keep busy, she thought as she wrestled a ladder from her utility closet. Anything to crowd out her thoughts of Nick and what they'd done in the library last night.

She must've gone temporarily insane. As if her life wasn't complicated enough! But all that sex stuff was out of her system now, she vowed. It was charmingly chivalrous that Nick had wanted to see her before she left the party, but she figured he was only doing his duty. He'd been every bit as quiet and withdrawn after their lovemaking as she—no doubt wondering how to slither out of a situation he hadn't really meant to get into.

She had just climbed up on the ladder with a wet piece of wallpaper when the doorbell rang.

"Oh, damn," she muttered. "Just a minute! I can't come to the door right this second...." She slapped a section of the border onto the wall. It was crooked and it had a big wrinkle in it. She tried smoothing it like in the "how to" diagram, but that only caused a new wrinkle. "Oh, hell's bells!"

"Bridget?" a concerned male voice called out through the door. "Are you all right in there?"

"Hold on, I'll be there in a minute." Omigod, what was Nick doing here on a Sunday morning? What was he doing here at all? She was wearing overalls, and her hair was pulled back in a scraggly ponytail.

She ripped the whole piece of wallpaper off the wall and tried placing it again, but her hands shook, and her results were worse than before.

She heard the front door creak open. "Bridget?"

"In here, in the spare bedroom."

TRYING TO TAMP DOWN his irrational panic, Nick strode toward the sound of Bridget's voice. He held a white paper bakery bag in one hand, containing two chocolate croissants, and Bridget's faux fur jacket in the other. When he rounded the corner into the bedroom and saw Bridget on a ladder wrestling with a piece of wallpaper about to swallow her, he dropped both croissants and jacket and rushed to her.

"Bridget, for heaven's sake, what are you doing up there?" He grabbed her around the knees with one hand and around her burgeoning middle with the other and carefully lifted her down to the floor amid sharp protests.

She pulled the wallpaper border out of her hair and glared at him. "Just what do you think you're doing?"

"Me? You were the one teetering up on that ladder. You almost gave me a heart attack."

"I was not teetering."

"What if you'd fallen? Aren't you worried about the baby?"

"I was being very careful. And yes, I worry about the baby all the time. Constantly. So spare me your... Do I smell chocolate?"

Nick quickly took advantage of the momentary distraction. "Chocolate croissants from Truelove's." He picked up the white bag he'd dropped and handed it to her, exchanging it for the ruined section of wallpaper. He pulled a pale wood rocking chair out from the wall and sat her in it. "Have you ever done wallpaper before?"

"No, but the guy at the store said it was easy."

"He was lying." Nick cut off the wrinkled, ruined part of the border and started fresh, repositioning the ladder, making sure the water and sponge were where he could reach them.

"You're going to paper my nursery?"

"I'm sure not letting you climb this ladder again."

"Bully. I happen to have excellent balance. I've never fallen off a ladder, and I wasn't planning to start today." But she didn't argue further. She sat in her chair and nibbled pastry while Nick struggled with the deceptively innocent border, which seemed to take on a life of its own as he battled it into submission with his mighty sponge.

It finally occurred to Bridget to ask what he was doing at her house on a Sunday morning.

"I'm returning your jacket. Mother asked me to. Well, no, that's not precisely true. I begged her to let me return it for her."

"You didn't need to manufacture an excuse to drop by." She sucked a smear of chocolate off her thumb, nearly causing Nick to fall off the ladder. Lips like hers should come with a warning label.

"You sure about that? You took some pains to avoid me last night. After the portrait unveiling, I looked everywhere for you. I asked Liz to find you for me. I even kept a watch on the front door so you couldn't slip out unnoticed. But apparently you still managed to."

"I wasn't feeling well," she told him, intently studying the last bite of her pastry. "Something disagreed with me. I was in no condition to socialize."

His concern for her welfare was immediate—and out of proportion, he knew. But he couldn't help it. He dropped the sponge into the bucket, leaving half a section of paper dangling down the wall. "You were sick?" From up on the ladder he studied her carefully, trying to find the slightest hint of illness—pallor, tremor, shadows under the eyes. But she looked in the pink of good health, thank God.

"Whatever it was, it was gone this morning," she said, dismissing his concern.

"It wasn't the sex that disagreed with you, was it?"

Bridget choked on something and started coughing. Nick was off the ladder and by her side immediately, but she waved him away. "Just a...pastry flake...gone down the wrong way."

He sprinted to the kitchen, found a glass, filled it from the tap and took it to her. She drank with a grateful nod.

"Mmm, I'm okay now. But give me a little warning next time you want to bring up that subject, okay?"

He hadn't meant to upset her. But even before he'd known she was sick, he'd worried that their activities had been too...strenuous for a woman in her condition. She was, by his calculations, about seven months along.

"You're sure we didn't do something we shouldn't have?"

"We may have done that, all right, but we certainly did nothing that was detrimental to the baby's health or mine. So you can stop looking so stricken."

He turned back to his task, more shaken by her casual words than he would have thought possible. "You regret what happened?"

She was silent so long he was forced to turn and look again, just to make sure she was still awake. She appeared deep in thought, her fingers steepled under her chin.

He worked on a particularly stubborn bubble under

the paper and waited for her to answer, for what seemed like several minutes.

"I don't regret it," she finally said.

That was it? No further explanation? "I don't, either," he said, trying to nudge the conversation along a bit. He didn't want to belabor the point, but he wanted to know her mind. If she didn't regret it, did that mean she wanted to repeat it?

"Good," was all she said.

He climbed down, moved the ladder, climbed up again. "I'm not into casual sex, despite what you might have heard about me."

"Oh? Then Saturday night was...a departure for you?"

He gave up on the damn wallpaper and climbed down. "It wasn't casual."

"Then it was committed?" she asked. "Because those are the only two kinds of sex I know about." Her calm awed him. How could she stay so cool when they were talking about something so important?

"There's caring." He knelt down and took her hand. The only indication that he had surprised her was a slight flaring of her nostrils. "We aren't in a position to commit right now. But that doesn't mean I can't care about you. Deeply, in fact. I wouldn't hurt you for the world, Bridget, and I've been worried that what we did might have been hurtful somehow, in ways besides the physical."

He was surprised to see moisture building in her eyes. "That's very sweet, Nick." She cleared her throat, turned away, then turned back. When she spoke again, her voice was less wavery. "But if we aren't in a position to commit right now, because of the baby, then we never will be. This child is mine for a lifetime. I've been entrusted with a human life that's a part of me, and I realize no man, not even a very good and kind one, is going to feel the same sense of commitment I do. How could you? The baby isn't yours. It doesn't carry your genes, your DNA.''

Every word she said was true. Yet they made him feel lower than armadillo toes. A woman having a baby *should* have that kind of commitment, and from a man she loves—and she'd be a fool to settle for less. She'd be a fool to settle for what he could give her.

"Well." He pushed himself to his feet. "That about says it, then."

"I appreciate your concern. You're a good man, Nick Raines, and I've enjoyed getting to know you. I'm glad we made love." Her smile was definitely a sad one. "But maybe it would be best if we said goodbye now, before the not-so-little watermelon makes his or her appearance. I would feel just sick if I thought you were hanging around out of some misplaced sense of duty or because you felt sorry for the poor single mom."

He struggled for something else to say, some graceful way to make his escape, now that she'd made her feelings clear. His gaze fell on the white bakery bag. Empty. He picked it up. "You ate both croissants? One of those was for me!"

"Oops. You should have told me. These days I'm eating everything that's not nailed down."

He shrugged. "Guess I'm not really hungry." He couldn't help himself. He cupped her face in his hand. "Take care of yourself. No more ladder climbing."

"Oh, all right."

"And you'll call me if there's anything I can do?"

"You could finish this blasted wallpaper."

He knew she didn't mean it. This was goodbye.
Quickly he zoomed in and snagged a kiss. Her lips
formed a surprised O just before he caught them, then
released them, taking with him the faint taste of chocolate. He turned and strode out of the room, out of
her life.

LIZ'S KNEES SHOOK as she stood before the front desk
at Statler Enterprises. The lobby looked like the inside of a spaceship, probably the most modern building in all of quaint Oaksboro, and the polished receptionist had a Jetsons hairstyle to match.

"Liz Van Zandt here to see Eric Statler."

The receptionist's eyes widened. "Do you have an
appointment?"

"No, but he knew I would be dropping by this
week sometime. I feel certain he'll want to see me."
She didn't feel certain at all, but she would have to
appear confident, as if she belonged here, if she was
going to get past the wall of protection this corporation's CEO had erected around him.

"I'll speak to his secretary," the receptionist said
dubiously.

Liz nodded and sat on one of the modular chairs.
It was hideously uncomfortable, doubtlessly designed
that way to discourage lingering.

A short time later the receptionist looked Liz's
way, her expression a tad warmer. "Sandra Burns,

Mr. Statler's secretary, is on her way down to get you. Sign in here, please.''

Liz signed in, clipped a visitor badge to her collar and allowed herself to be led upstairs by an unsmiling bulldog of a woman who didn't introduce herself and, in fact, avoided conversation completely. Liz wondered if this was the one who always answered the phone and never put her calls through.

The bulldog showed Liz into a small waiting area featuring the same uncomfortable chairs as the lobby, put a cup of coffee in front of her without asking and told her Mr. Statler was in a meeting and would be with her whenever he could break free.

That was encouraging, Liz thought, clutching her manila envelope full of papers in one tight, clammy hand. At least he hadn't had security escort her off the grounds.

He did make her wait, though. She wondered if he was legitimately tied up or if he was playing some kind of power game with her. She decided to give him the benefit of the doubt. He was a CEO, after all. He probably had a full schedule.

After twenty minutes, the waiting room door opened and Eric entered, looking polished as ever in a suit that probably cost more than Liz's entire closet. What really mattered, though, was the look on his face, which Liz studied closely in the split seconds she had before they started speaking. He didn't seem angry. In fact, he looked—unsure of himself. She didn't recall ever seeing Eric appear less than 100 percent confident.

"Liz. Sorry to make you wait." He stood awkwardly in the doorway, obviously unsure what reception he would get.

She tried to gloss over the awkward moment with a smile. "No problem. I took my chances, dropping in unannounced. But I've not had much luck trying to get to you through your army of secretaries."

"I'm sorry for that. They go overboard trying to protect me sometimes."

Liz nodded toward the door. "Can we close that, please?"

"Sure." He pushed it shut. She sat down in the same chair she'd occupied before, and he sat across from her. All very cordial. So far, so good. Her lawyer had made her promise not to get emotional or lose her temper and say things that might get her into more hot water, and she was determined to remain cool and businesslike. From the look of things, Eric didn't want a scene, either.

"Is this room completely private?" she asked.

"Yes. Sandra knows we're here, and she won't let anyone interrupt us. I can clear my schedule for the rest of the day if you want. Obviously we need to talk."

She was surprised by his accommodating attitude. When last they'd seen each other, he hadn't been at all interested in conversation. All he'd wanted to do was hurl insults and character assassinations. She decided it would serve no purpose to remind him of that.

"This shouldn't take too long," she said, opening the envelope and pulling out a thin sheaf of papers. "I had a lawyer draw up some papers…" At the mention of the word *lawyer*, a muscle in Eric's cheek jumped, but he didn't say anything. "Basically," she continued, "this is a contract absolving you of all responsibility for my unborn child. In return I'm asking you to sever all parental rights. There are also a couple of clauses having to do with confidentiality. Since it's not in either of our best interests to bandy about the biological parentage of my child, I'm sure you won't have a problem with that."

She laid the document on the coffee table between them and gave it a gentle push. "I don't expect you to sign it here and now, of course. I know you'll want your own attorney to look it over, but it's pretty cut-and-dried."

Eric made no move to take the contract, staring at it as if she'd tossed a dead animal onto the table. Then he looked at her. "You're going to deny your child a father?"

"That's what you want, right? Besides, maybe he or she will have a father some day. If I ever find the right man." She sighed wistfully, just so Eric would know she did not, in any way, consider him the right man.

"No way."

Her gaze snapped back to him. "You might be right. Good men are hard to find, good fathers even harder."

"No, I mean, my child will never, ever, call some other guy Daddy." With deliberate movements he picked up the contract the lawyer had so carefully worded, the one she'd paid three hundred of her hard-earned dollars to have drafted, and tore it into a hundred pieces.

"Eric, what are you doing?" The first stabs of panic sliced through her.

"We'll draw up a new agreement, one that involves reasonable—no, make that generous—child-support payments."

"But I just told you I don't want money from you. I'm letting you off the hook."

"I don't *want* off the hook." He tossed the contract shreds onto the table.

"But last Saturday you said you didn't want a family!"

"I believe I said I wouldn't be a good husband. Anyway, that was before I knew about Eric IV."

Liz resisted the urge to leap across the space separating them and go for Eric's throat. "Over my dead body is this kid going to be called Four." She shuddered. "What in heaven's name suddenly makes you think you'll be a good father?"

His confidence faltered. "I don't know about a *good* father. But I deserve the chance to try, don't I?"

She took a deep breath and ordered herself not to reply in anger. This wasn't going exactly as she'd planned. "Through an accident in biology you managed to contribute some chromosomes to my baby. And you want some kind of medal for that?"

"The same biological accident that made you the baby's mother," he reminded her.

"Yes, but I've been planning for this my whole life. Three days ago you were so horrified by the prospect of fatherhood, I think you'd have jumped out of an airplane without a parachute to escape from it."

"I'm not proud of the way I treated you Saturday night. Your news took me by surprise, to say the least, and I apologize for my less than graceful reaction."

"Less than graceful?" She came out of her chair. She couldn't help it, calm-and-cool be damned. "You called me a gold digger."

"I didn't use that word."

"You might as well have." This arguing was getting them nowhere. She clasped her hands in front of her and made herself sit down. "Please, Eric. I know you're a decent man. But if my baby has a father, I want him to be a full-time, dedicated, live-in father, not somebody who has to drag himself away from the office to grudgingly honor a visitation schedule. You don't really want or need a child in your life."

"I didn't think I did. But now that there is one…I can't turn my back."

Liz steeled her determination. "You have to. I'm not giving you a choice." It was the wrong thing to say. Eric was not a man to back down when challenged.

"You're wrong, Liz. The baby is mine as much as yours. Either agree to reasonable visitation, or find yourself on the receiving end of a child custody suit."

Liz felt as if she'd been hit on the head with a mallet. "You will not take this baby away. No court in the world would take a child away from a dedicated mother and give it to a man who works twenty-four hours a day!"

"Really? I've got more and meaner lawyers than you and deeper pockets. Do you really care to entrust your child's future to our fair and reasonable court system?''

"Damn you! What about your father? How will he feel about an unplanned grandchild?"

She could see she'd hit a vulnerable spot, but he covered it up pretty quickly. "Two will have to understand. Anyway, he wants grandchildren."

"I'll run away," she said without much conviction.

"I'll find you!"

The scary thing was, he would do it. "You really hate to lose, don't you."

"I don't know. I've never lost."

Liz stood up, threw her purse strap over her shoulder and headed for the door. "Yes, you have. You've lost any shred of respect I ever had for you."

ERIC WATCHED HER LEAVE, feeling utterly helpless. He'd thought the situation between him and Liz couldn't get any worse after their last meeting, but it had.

Sandra poked her head through the doorway. "Mr. Statler, that woman just roared past my station. I tried to stop her, but—"

"It's all right, Sandra."

"But she's a visitor. She can't just wander through the building without an escort! Should I call security?"

Tempting, to have a couple of beefy security guards catch Liz, hold her down and make her listen to reason. But he'd already thrown his weight around with Liz, and it wasn't having the desired effect. "Just let her go."

"All right, if you say so." Sandra started to withdraw, then changed her mind and came all the way into the room. "Are you all right, Mr. Statler?"

He forced some enthusiasm. "Never better. Sandra, are you married?"

His secretary did something he'd rarely seen her do: she smiled. "Why, yes, sir. Twenty-eight years next May."

"Kids?"

"Two grown sons. And a grandbaby on the way. Why do you ask?"

He wasn't sure. Maybe it was because he was afraid Liz was more stubborn than he was. Maybe it was because he was very afraid he would never know his offspring.

The threat he'd made to Liz was an empty one. He would never drag her through court or impoverish her with the expenses of a legal defense. If she really, really wanted to keep their son or daughter to herself, she could do it. In fact, after the way he'd been acting, he couldn't really blame her.

But he held on to a slim hope that she would see reason and let him participate. He could be a good father, if he put his mind to it. It was all a matter of priorities. He couldn't explain it, but in the past few days his unborn child had become the most important thing in his life, with the child's mother running a close second.

After screwing up so badly, how could he ever make Liz understand that?

Chapter Thirteen

Bridget pushed her grocery cart through the Shop'N'Save, trying to drum up some enthusiasm for her mother's annual Super Bowl party. Even when the Dallas Cowboys weren't playing, Sophie Van Zandt invited everyone she knew to come watch the spectacle on her big-screen TV and partake in a lavish spread.

As was customary, Bridget and Liz were doing the shopping for the extravaganza, though Bridget felt more sluggish with each passing day. She had six weeks left to endure, and the only thing she could find to be grateful for was that it wasn't summer. Poor Liz would be delivering *her* child in August.

"Should we get the extra-hot Rotel tomatoes for the dip," Liz asked, "or just the normal hot?"

"Normal hot," Bridget answered. "Last year we just about burned off Aunt Hazel's taste buds with the extra-hot."

"Right. Okay, what's left?"

"Pearl onions. Where do they keep those? I can never re— Oh, my God."

"What?"

"Over there, in the potato chip aisle. Do you see what I see?"

Liz looked, then gasped. "What are *they* doing in a grocery store?"

"Arguing over chips, it looks like. They must be having a Super Bowl party, too."

"And they don't have servants to do the shopping?"

"Nick doesn't have any servants. Maybe it's his party. Liz, stop staring. They'll see us." Bridget turned her cart down the next aisle.

"Would that be so bad?"

"Yes! Or did I get it wrong, and that's *not* the guy who wants to take your child away from you?"

"I was thinking about Nick. And you. Maybe you need to talk again."

Bridget grabbed an extra large jar of black olives and put it in the cart. "It'll just make things harder."

"But he seems so nice."

"He is nice. He's just not cut out for family life. At least Eric was willing to accept responsibility."

"Eric wants to control everything. That's different than accepting responsibility. Anyway, Nick seems very responsible. I bet once he saw your kid—"

"It won't happen."

"How can you say that? Oaksboro is a small town. You'll run into him. Just like now."

"In a few months that won't matter. I'll be completely over him, and we can exchange a few pleasantries and be on our way."

"But you're not over him yet."

Bridget sighed. "I just…"

"What?" They'd stopped their cart in the middle

of the aisle so that an elderly woman had to maneuver around them.

Bridget mumbled an apology and scooted the cart to the side. "Sometimes I do think about what it would be like to have a traditional family—you know, mom, dad, kids." More often than not, Nick's face was part of that fantasy.

"Yeah, me too," Liz said wistfully. "Families like that are in the minority now, you know."

"Really?"

"Yeah. Mom did okay raising us alone. What we're doing is completely normal."

"Then why do I feel so deviant sometimes?"

"Uh-oh, don't look now, but we have company."

Bridget put the cart in gear and hightailed it to the next aisle.

"C'mon, Bridget, just talk to him. I'll lure Eric away."

Bridget laughed. "How? Offer to have another argument with him?"

"We don't always argue," Liz said, patting her still-flat tummy. "In fact, we communicate quite well…when the lights are off."

"Then maybe you and the lawyers should negotiate in a cellar."

Bridget worked her way through the rest of the awesome grocery list in record time, craving escape, not to mention rest for her swollen ankles. But when she reached the checkout lines, she realized she was a long way from escape.

"Jeez, what a zoo," Liz said. "I guess we aren't the only ones in town stocking up for the Super Bowl."

Bridget chose the shortest line and hunkered down for the long wait. She amused herself by reading tabloid headlines while Liz thumbed through *Cosmopolitan.*

Gradually Bridget became aware of a disturbing presence invading her aura. Okay, she didn't believe in auras, but that was how it felt. Cautiously she looked up and found Nick staring at her from the next line over.

"Bridget. Imagine meeting you here."

"Hi, Nick." She pasted on what felt like a hideously fake smile.

Apparently she and Nick weren't the only ones who'd discovered each other. Eric and Liz were staring at each other as if nothing else in the universe existed.

Liz tapped Bridget's shoulder. "We forgot the aluminum foil." Abruptly she turned and strode away.

Nick nudged Eric in the ribs. "We forgot beer nuts."

"No, we didn't," Eric argued, pointing into the full cart. "They're right—"

"Cashews, then."

Eric finally got the hint. "Cashews, right." He wandered off.

"How are you doing?" Nick asked.

"Fine," came Bridget's automatic answer.

"Come on. How are you really doing?"

Bridget found she couldn't lie. "I feel like Shamu the Killer Whale."

"Well you look…fantastic."

"Liar."

"It's the truth. How much longer do you have?"

"Six weeks." Bridget moved her cart up a couple of feet as the line advanced.

Nick's line moved, too, keeping him even with her. "I've been thinking about you a lot."

Bridget said nothing to this, but she gave him a look that said she was open to hearing more. Lord knew she'd been obsessed with thoughts of him.

"Mostly I've been thinking of something you said to me at my mother's party."

"I probably said a lot of dumb things that night. My hormones were running amok." She'd found the old hormone defense to be a handy excuse for her bad behavior these last few months.

"You said you and Liz were willing to have children without fathers because no men were standing in line to marry you. I have a hard time believing you, but I don't suppose you have any reason to lie about that."

She glanced around to see if anyone was listening to them, but everyone appeared involved in their own conversation.

"Gee, thanks. I think."

"But now that I've thought about it, I see your point. I'd like to have kids someday."

She looked at him sharply.

"Well, most men, if they're honest, want kids. They want to leave a legacy and all that. But we have our whole lives to do it. We can have kids when we're forty, fifty. It's harder for women."

"Well, duh. Fertility drops drastically for a woman in her thirties." Bridget had read that statistic so many times it made her head hurt. "Is there a point here?"

"I just wanted you to know that I've been thinking about your position. And I understand why you did it. It's not a choice I would personally make—"

"I don't believe you could be artificially inseminated, anyway."

"—but I was wrong to criticize your decision without knowing anything of the circumstances, and I apologize. I know you'll be a good mother."

She had to give him credit. It was a rare man who could swallow his pride and admit he was wrong. She smiled—a real smile, this time. "Apology accepted."

"That said, I think there's a way you can do better."

"Oh?" Bridget's hackles rose. What judgment was he going to impose on her now?

"Marry me."

All of the blood in Bridget's head drained to her feet. Again she looked around nervously, but no one paid them the slightest bit of attention. "Did...did you just propose to me in a *supermarket?*"

"I'm talking about a practical arrangement. Your baby needs a name and a father figure."

"Van Zandt is a perfectly good name!"

Nick continued, undaunted, speaking in a low, reasonable voice. "You and I are compatible—I think we've proved that. And I've gotten sort of attached to the idea of meeting your little watermelon when he or she comes into the world."

"Attached?"

"I'm reasonably stable even though I buy and sell a lot of companies, and financially I'm completely sound. I own my house outright. I'll let you look at my tax returns."

"Financially...sound." Bridget's head started to buzz.

"In return, you would provide me with stability and...and a better reason to work hard. Something to come home to at night. My mother already adores you and would welcome you into the family, watermelon and all."

"And your stepfather?" she couldn't help asking.

"Oh, he'll adjust. So, how about it?"

"We're in a grocery store!"

"I'm a man who grabs opportunity when it presents itself."

"Paper or plastic?" the checkout clerk asked Bridget.

"Uh, paper. No, plastic! Oh, I don't know. Whatever you have the most of."

The clerk gave her a strange look, then started unloading the basket.

Bridget was appalled to realize she was actually thinking about Nick's offer. No matter how unappealingly he'd just stated his case, marriage to Nick was not something to be dismissed out of hand. Hadn't she dreamed about it, in unguarded moments?

"Are these oranges or tangelos?" the checker asked.

"Uh, oranges." Bridget looked back over her shoulder at Nick, who'd fallen behind her. Several feet and an impulse-candy aisle separated them. But this wasn't a conversation that could be halted in the middle. "Answer me this, Nick," she said, loud enough that everybody in both lines could hear. "Where's the love in this arrangement?"

All conversation stopped.

Nick stared at her. "I do love you, Bridget."

A couple of people in line applauded. Bridget wasn't one of them. She'd had to force the declaration out of him, and he'd had to say it. Maybe he even meant it. But she wasn't so worried about herself. She wanted him to love the child. And he'd said nothing about that.

"It's $62.20," the checker said, then whispered, "Take him up on the offer, honey. I wouldn't let that one get away, especially in your condition."

Bridget wanted to punch her—Shamu surfacing again—but she bit her tongue, handed the checker exact change, grabbed her cart. She looked over her shoulder at Nick. "Thanks, but I don't think so."

As Liz READ about the tensile strengths of various aluminum foils, someone touched her on the shoulder. She whirled around and was face-to-face with Eric, who carried a jar of dry-roasted cashews.

"We need to talk."

"Talk to my lawyer." She tried to walk past him, but he stepped in front of her.

"I don't even know your lawyer's name."

"You would if you hadn't torn up the contract. Her name was on it."

"If we involve a bunch of lawyers, they're the only ones who'll come out ahead. Why can't we work this out like rational adults?"

"Because one of us isn't rational. One of us thinks this is a game he has to win."

"We can both win."

"And what about the child? What does he get?

Please, Eric, if you have any feelings at all for me or the baby, don't do this to us. Let us live in peace.''

"Don't I get any peace? I want to be part of my child's life. I want him or her to have the best of everything.''

"The best of everything doesn't include a father who doesn't have time for him.''

"I would make time.''

"A few weeks ago your company was the most important thing in your life. You came out and told me that even if I agreed to be your kept woman, you wouldn't have much time for me. *And* you wanted to keep our relationship a secret. You can't keep a child secret.''

"I wouldn't want to. But I have to be careful how I break the news to Two.''

"You don't really think news of a grandchild will kill him, do you?''

Eric shook his head. "Two is actually doing much better, now that he's retired. His blood pressure's lower than it's been in years. But…''

"What?''

"When I was in college, a girl I'd dated a few times accused me of getting her pregnant. I hadn't even slept with Kelly. But she put on a pretty convincing show, and it upset my father terribly. That was when he had his first heart attack.''

Liz thought Eric couldn't possibly shock her, but he just had. No wonder the man was sensitive about paternity suits. "Oh, Eric.'' She couldn't help feeling sorry for the bewildered young man he must have been.

"Two paid the girl off just to keep the story quiet.

The look of disappointment in his eyes was awful to see."

"But you didn't do anything!"

"Except show bad judgment. I shouldn't have dated Kelly. I knew why she wanted to go out with me. She had dollar signs in her eyes."

Liz studied a box of garbage bags. "Getting me pregnant probably wasn't the smartest thing you've ever done, either."

"Maybe not. But I'm entitled to a lapse in judgment now and then. Everybody is. Two will just have to accept that my priorities have changed. I'm prepared to make this child the most important thing in my life. Still, I didn't want to make any announcements to the family until you and I have come to an agreement."

She narrowed her eyes. "Is the child so important you would take him away from his mother?"

"Those were idle threats, Liz. I would *never* take your baby away…no matter how unfair you're being."

"Unfair? You want unfair?" Liz's temper rose again. "A kid with a mother and father who live in separate houses and use him for a battleground. Haven't you known kids like that? A childhood spent getting dragged from one house to another, splitting up holidays and vacations, trying to please both, trying to spread out love so both parents feel like they're getting enough? *That's* unfair."

"It wouldn't be like that with our child."

"Damn right. You hear me good, Eric Statler. If you want to be a father, then you be a full-time one."

"How do you propose I do that?"

"Marry me, how else?"

Finally she'd stunned him into silence. He stared at her as if contemplating having her committed, and did she blame him? She'd said it for the shock value, nothing more. She wouldn't marry Eric Statler if he were the last man in all of Texas.

Taking advantage of his momentary muteness, she walked around him and headed quickly for the exit, leaving the box of foil on an animal cracker display. She hadn't really needed foil, anyway.

"So DID YOU TALK TO LIZ?" Nick asked as Eric guided his Range Rover out of the crowded supermarket parking lot.

"She's insane."

"We've established that. Did you accomplish anything? Did you tell her you wouldn't sue her for custody? Jeez, I can't believe you threatened that in the first place. Didn't Mom ever teach you about flies and honey and vinegar?"

"I told her. I was completely reasonable, completely understanding. I poured out my heart to her, standing right there in the garbage bag aisle of Shop'N'Save. And you know what the crazy woman did?"

"What?"

"She proposed to me."

"As in marriage?"

"Yeah. What kind of deranged person proposes marriage in a supermarket?"

Nick cleared his throat and fiddled with the buttons for the heater. "Must be those fluorescent lights. What did you say?"

"I didn't say anything. I was too shocked. Then she walked away."

"Smooth. What do you want to say?"

"I'm not going to marry some woman just because she's pregnant."

"Then how about you marry her because you're crazy in love with her?"

Eric ran the Range Rover onto the curb and nearly hit a fire hydrant. Once he'd put the vehicle back properly on the road, he pulled over and cut the engine. "I am not in love with Liz Van Zandt. I mean, sure she's gorgeous and smart and funny and I'm wildly attracted to her, and I'm thinking she'll still be beautiful even when she has a stomach as big as her sister's, and we couldn't be more compatible physically, but..." He turned doleful eyes on Nick. "Oh, my God, I *am* in love with her."

"So marry her," Nick said with that annoyingly certain big-brother voice of his.

"Like, it's that easy?" Eric restarted his car. "She doesn't really want to marry me. She's bluffing."

"Call her bluff, then."

"If I could just talk to her without one of us getting mad and stomping off."

"You could try just telling her how you really feel."

"Tell her I love her? Do you know how much power that would give her over me?"

Nick punched Eric on the arm. "This isn't a hostile corporate takeover. It's the rest of your life."

NICK TRIED to cheer himself up watching the Super Bowl. Geraldine, never one to overlook an excuse for a party, had invited over family and a few friends to watch and gorge themselves on chips and cheese balls. She did it every year, even if the game was between two teams no one cared about. Ordinarily Nick found the antics of his eccentric family amusing. But this year he couldn't get his mind off Bridget long enough to laugh at cousin Harry walking around with two Pringles chips stuck over his eyes.

Once Geraldine was sure everyone had a beverage and the smoked turkey was sliced, she came and perched on the sofa arm next to Nick. "You're awfully somber today," she said quietly, rubbing his shoulder. "Is anything wrong? Two hasn't been needling you, has he?"

"You know he doesn't get to me anymore. Much."

"I hardly spoke to him for a week after that business with the portrait. Imagine wanting to shuttle your picture off to the music room. I set him straight on that, you know."

He knew. He'd seen the picture hung in the library.

"If it's not Two, then what? I could always tell when something was bothering one of my boys."

"Eric's the one who's cranky."

"He won't talk to me, either," Geraldine said glumly. "You boys used to tell me everything."

Nick slid an arm around his mother. "Some things a mom just can't fix." Like the fact that Nick had proposed marriage to a woman in a supermarket and declared his love so tentatively she didn't believe him. Like the fact he'd made such a big deal about what lousy father material he was that she likely wouldn't let him within a hundred feet of her kid.

And Eric. He'd finally found a woman who could lure him away from that damn company, and what did he do? Got her pregnant the first time out of the chute, treated her like some common street tart, then threatened to take her kid away. Nick couldn't imagine what Eric did to women he *didn't* love.

As the second quarter drew to a close, Eric paced the TV room like a caged tiger. He didn't even notice when the underdog Vikings made a spectacular interception, ran the ball for sixty yards and tied up the score.

The teams headed for the locker rooms, and Eric seized the remote control and muted the TV.

"Hey, I want to see the halftime show," their teenage cousin Belinda complained.

"You can wait a few minutes. I have something I want to tell the family, while everyone's in one place."

Oh, Lord, Nick thought. Surely Eric wasn't doing what Nick thought he was doing.

All conversation stilled.

"What's the problem, Son?" Two asked, putting his hand on Eric's shoulder. "Whatever it is, you know we'll support you 100 percent."

"I guess there's no other way to say it. I'm having a baby."

Nick's cousin Diana immediately pushed Belinda out the door. "Go watch the halftime show on the TV upstairs."

"You're spinning off another subsidiary?" Two asked hopefully.

"No," Eric said, "I'm talking about a real baby. Liz Van Zandt is the mother."

Two's eyes bulged out of his head. "The girl who tried to steal your mother's Japanese fan?"

"Oh, now, Two, Nick explained that to me," Geraldine said quickly. "She just borrowed it for a few minutes to hide her face."

"Well, she ought to hide her face. I suppose now she's going to try to get money out of us."

"Oh, Two, hush up." Geraldine hopped off her perch on the sofa, went to Eric and hugged him. "I've always wanted to be a grandmother. You're going to marry her, aren't you?"

"Marry her?" Two roared. "You are not marrying some two-bit gold digger who trapped you into—"

"She did not trap me," Eric said, his eyes blazing with outrage. "She doesn't even want child support. In fact, she'd like to be rid of me."

"Then maybe you should oblige her," Two said, calming a bit. "She's not the sort of woman you want attached to you for the rest of your life."

"And just what sort of woman would be better?" Geraldine argued, putting her arm around Eric. "One of those empty-headed little debutantes you're always throwing at Eric?"

"Somebody with a few connections and decent bloodlines, at least," Two grumbled.

"We're not talking racehorses, we're talking people, you old coot. Or have you forgotten what a hassle your parents gave you when you wanted to marry an uneducated single woman with a kid in tow and not a speck of blue in her blood?"

Nick shook his head and stifled a laugh. This was better than a Super Bowl halftime show anyday.

"That was different," Two said.

"It doesn't matter," Eric said. "I don't believe Liz and I will be getting married."

"Why not?" Nick asked. "She proposed to you in the Shop'N'Save."

Geraldine gasped. "Why, Eric, if she wants to marry you, then you have to do the right thing! Didn't I raise you to take responsibility for your actions?"

Eric gave Nick the evil eye. "Thanks a lot, Brother."

"No charge."

"This is the thanks I get for entrusting my company to you, Eric?" Two asked. "If you preoccupy yourself with a woman and a child now, at this critical time, Statler Enterprises will go to hell in a handbasket!"

"Then maybe you should give the company to someone else. Because I would like to have a life."

"You would just throw away the years of dedication—"

"Two, remember your blood pressure," Geraldine cautioned.

"All those years of dedication may have cost me the best thing that's ever happened to me." With that, Eric stormed out of the room.

"I'll disinherit the boy," Two declared.

"You've disinherited everybody else," Geraldine grumbled, "including me, seven times. I don't see why Eric should be any different."

Nick smiled at his mother. "He'll make a good father, huh?"

"I've always thought *you* would make me a grandmother first."

"Don't count me out yet."

Chapter Fourteen

Two weeks had passed since Nick's encounter with Bridget at the grocery store. He'd held on to a slender hope that she might change her mind and agree to marry him, or at least invite him back into her life. But he hadn't heard a peep out of her.

It was time to be proactive. He would talk with her again and somehow convince her that not only did he love her, he loved a kid he hadn't even laid eyes on. He'd held Bridget during her morning sickness, he'd catered to her bizarre cravings, he'd watched her body ripen, he'd helped her decorate her nursery. And somehow, without his realizing it, the two of them had gotten under his skin.

If the child were from his own body, he wouldn't feel any more strongly.

It was a Saturday morning, bitterly cold since a "blue norther'" had blown in the night before. Finally Oaksboro was getting some proper winter weather. The weatherman had even mentioned snow, though the town hadn't seen frozen white stuff in years.

He would drop by Bridget's and check to see that

her furnace was working right. He would take her a bag of salt for her front steps and driveway, in case of icing. He would take her a load of firewood and make sure her fireplace vented properly. He had all kinds of excuses to see her.

There was just one problem: she wasn't home. He called first, to see if she would answer the phone, and her voice mail came on the line.

"This is Bridget Van Zandt of Moving Pictures, Inc. Please leave a detailed message, and I'll get back to you. If you really need to speak to me, you can reach me at…" And she rattled off a number. Her mother's? He wouldn't blame her for not wanting to stay alone during these last few weeks of pregnancy.

He dialed the number, and Bridget herself answered. "Red Fox Galleries."

Now he remembered. She was a member of a co-op art gallery that displayed her landscapes and still lifes, and she worked there on Saturdays.

He pinched his nose shut, raised his voice two octaves, and put on a foreign accent. "Sorry, wrong number." Then he cursed himself for acting like a juvenile. Still, he didn't want to talk to her on the phone. She might forbid him from coming to see her, and what he had to say had to be said in person.

As he drove his truck toward the old town square where the gallery was located, a light sleet began pelting his windshield. A bank thermometer declared it to be twenty-two degrees.

Bridget shouldn't be out in this, he thought. She ought to be home in front of a roaring fire with an afghan wrapped around her, sipping hot cider.

Never mind that the inviting mental picture featured himself sitting next to her with his own cup of cider. Maybe they were talking in drowsy voices about their child's future or something more mundane like next summer's vacation plans.

He had no idea how one woman had tied him into such domestic knots, but that fantasy picture in his head was so delicious he knew he had to have it. And, by God, he was going to get it. He would make Bridget understand somehow.

Several open parking places beckoned to him. Not many shoppers out today. Maybe he could talk Bridget into closing the gallery—surely no one would mind—and coming home with him.

He entered the little brick-front gallery, stamping bits of ice from his shoes and shaking off the cold.

"Be with you in a minute."

His heart lifted at the sound of her voice. Then it came up into his throat. Bridget was standing on a ladder! Again! She was measuring a space on the wall and making marks with a pencil.

Nick didn't want to startle her, so he very softly and reasonably said, "Don't you think it's a little dangerous for you to be up there?"

"I have excellent balance," she replied, just as she'd said that day at her house, sounding completely unconcerned.

He came a little closer, watching for any misstep. She seemed steady enough, so he let her be. For once, he wasn't going to bulldoze his way through Bridget's life, though he was ready to spring into action if that ladder wobbled even a fraction of an inch.

He kept his gaze riveted to her feet. It was better

this way, he decided. He was afraid he couldn't say what he needed to say while looking her in the eye. "I had to see you, Bridget."

"Um, Nick?"

"No, don't say anything, just hear me out. These last two weeks have been pure misery. I've said everything, done everything all wrong where you're concerned, but I want to make things right. I love you, and I love your baby. I want it to be *our* baby, and I want brothers and sisters for him or her, a whole houseful if you're willing. I'll be the best damn father—"

"Nick!"

"Don't answer me now. I know I haven't given you any reason to believe I'd be a good husband or father, but I intend to spend the rest of my life proving myself, if that's what it takes. I love you, Bridget, and I want to marry you."

The front door of the gallery jangled. Annoyed, Nick looked toward the intrusive sound. This time, his heart dropped to his feet. Walking through the door was Bridget, complete with a stomach so big it wouldn't fit under her coat.

Which meant that the woman on the ladder... He chanced a glance up just as Liz stepped down. She'd had her back to him before, but still, how could he have missed the fact that she didn't have a resident watermelon?

Bridget just stared.

"Oops," Nick said, looking at Liz, hoping she could somehow salvage this mess.

Liz laughed. "Bridget, thank God you're back. This poor man is obviously painfully in love with you, and you'd better do something about it." She headed for the exit, grabbing her purse and coat from a rack near the door. "Did Dr. Keller say you're okay?"

Bridget nodded.

"Good. I'd love to stay and see how this all turns out, but I'm late for a hair appointment. Ta!"

Nick put a hand to his forehead. It had taken a lot of courage to say what he'd just said to Liz. He didn't know how he would manage to repeat it, but he had to. "I thought she was you."

"She was filling in for me while I went to a doctor's appointment."

"I wasted all my best lines on her."

Bridget's face softened. "Oh, Nick..."

"I know, I should have realized it was Liz. But I was expecting to find you here, not your sister." He closed the distance between them, but stopped short of taking Bridget in his arms. She wasn't ready for that. Instead he helped her off with her coat. "How was your doctor's appointment?"

"I feel awful, but the doctor said everything is fine. Nick, what are you doing here?"

"I came here to convince you I love you. And the baby. I had all sorts of persuasive arguments memorized. Unfortunately, I used them all on the wrong twin." He took her hand and led her to the small antique desk in the middle of the gallery. The matching chair looked almost too dainty to hold Bridget, but he made her sit down, anyway.

She'd made no reply to his declaration. In fact, he wasn't sure she'd heard him. She seemed preoccupied.

The sense of urgency he'd felt earlier to speak his mind was replaced by concern for Bridget. She looked pale and tired. "You need to rest, Bridget. Why don't you close up the gallery and let me take you home? I'll make you some hot cider," he added.

"I'll be fine. If the weather gets much worse I'll take your advice, but otherwise I need to keep the gallery open. We do little enough business as it is."

Nick looked around at the paintings, among them the wine bottle still life he'd admired in her studio all those weeks ago. It was stunning, but so were some of the others. He easily spotted Bridget's work from among the rest.

If he offered to buy all of her paintings, would she take the rest of the day off? He decided she wouldn't appreciate his meddling.

"Are you taking childbirth classes?" he asked instead.

"Yes, at the hospital. Liz has been coming with me."

"Oh. Then you don't need a coach."

"Not unless it comes with four horses and a fairy godmother."

He studied her. The strain showed on her face, around her mouth. "What would you ask the fairy godmother to do?"

"I'd ask her if I could skip this last month and go right to the delivery. I'm really tired of carrying around this...this Volkswagen!" She started sobbing.

He was by her side in an instant. "Bridget, Bridget, don't cry, please, I can't stand it. Everything's going to be all right."

She leaned into his embrace, resting her cheek

against his sweater. "I know. I'm not being a very good sport about this. I'm supposed to be strong and brave and happy, but I'm exhausted all the time and scared and cowardly. I want this baby so badly, but I never knew I'd have so many doubts...."

"I'm sure that's natural. You don't have to be brave around me. I'm scared, too."

"Why are you scared?"

"Are you kidding? I'm terrified. When I think about you living all alone, and something going wrong—" He stopped himself. He should be reassuring her, not adding to her fears. "The thing I'm most scared about, though, is that you won't let me be there with you when it happens."

"You want to be?" she asked, sounding awed.

"I want to be a part of your life. From this moment on I don't want to miss anything. I want to marry you, and I want the baby to be mine. Emotionally, legally, whatever it takes."

"Oh, Nick!" She hugged him tightly. "I think...I mean, if we get married right away, then we won't have to bother with adoption or anything like that."

"Was that a yes?"

She pulled away and looked into his eyes. Her cheeks were tear-stained and her eyes red, but she'd never looked more beautiful to him. "Yes. I love you so much, I've loved you for months and I should've said yes at the grocery store."

Nick felt the pangs of humiliation. "That was the stinkiest proposal of all time. You were right to walk away. You forced me to do better."

"You did fine." She brought her mouth to his in the gentlest of kisses.

"Let's fly to Vegas and get married."

"Nick, I can't fly anywhere."

"Oh, right. Then we'll go to city hall first thing Monday morning and get the license and the blood test and whatever else is required, and we'll be married by the end of the week."

"But no wedding pictures. Not unless they're from the neck up."

"What about a wedding night?"

"You'd want to?"

"You're beautiful and sexy and you turn me on."

She looked down at where her toes used to be. They were only a distant memory now. "I don't think I can."

Nick shrugged. "Then we'll wait."

"Oh, my God, you really do love me." She started to throw her arms around him again, but stopped halfway there, looking confused.

"Bridget?"

"Ah, it's…it's nothing." She smiled, but the smile immediately faded. "No, wait, it's something."

"What?"

"It's like a…ahhhhh!" She let out a bellow that sounded like a cow caught in a barbwire fence, scaring the dickens out of Nick.

He reached for the phone on the desk. "I'm calling 9-1-1."

She grabbed his arm. "No, really, that's not necessary. I've been having these pains all morning. That's why I went to the doctor. But he was quite sure I'm not in labor."

"If not labor, then what? It can't be normal."

"False labor. I guess my body's sort of practicing

for the real thing." She didn't look entirely convinced. "But that was the worst one yet."

"What's your doctor's phone number?" he asked. "We'll call him again."

"Won't do any good. He was leaving for a ski vacation right after my appointment."

"Figures. Does he have an associate?"

"Yes, but I don't want to bother some strange doctor—" She stopped, and that curious look came over her face again. She didn't cry out this time, but she squeezed her eyes shut and gripped the chair arms until Nick was sure they'd break off.

"That does it. I'm taking you to the hospital."

"I don't think—"

"Well, I do. I'm not taking any chances with my future wife—or my child. If it's a false alarm, we'll just look a little foolish and we'll go home."

Somehow she managed a radiant smile. "All right. I guess no one will be shopping for a painting in this weather, anyway."

As BRIDGET PUT ON HER COAT, she looked outside. The white stuff was coming down in sheets now, sleet mixed with snow. She couldn't believe how much the weather had deteriorated in just the few minutes she'd been inside the gallery.

"How does your car drive on the ice?" she asked.

"I don't know," Nick admitted. "We haven't had an ice storm since before I bought it. But it's got front-wheel drive. Maybe we should take yours."

"It doesn't have four-wheel, either. And the tires are almost bald."

"Bridget!"

"I've had a lot on my plate, okay? New tires are next on my list."

Nick opened the door, letting the biting wind in. She hurried through it, then almost slipped on the sidewalk.

Nick grabbed her just in time. "Hold on to me. Those flimsy shoes you've got on aren't meant for sleet."

She was more than glad to grab on to his sturdy arm as she turned the sign on the door to Closed, then shut and locked the door. She was glad to have his sturdy presence in general. She was, in fact, more than happy to let the man take charge. She was so tired of dealing with everything alone. Though Liz and her mother were always there for her, the important decisions always came down to her.

With a minimum of fuss, Nick got her into his truck and buckled her in. Then he climbed in himself, got the heater going and backed carefully out of the parking spot. His tires, thank God, seemed to be gripping the street.

He didn't have to ask what hospital. Oaksboro only had one.

"You're not to full term yet, are you?" Nick asked quietly.

"I have twenty-six days to go."

"Twenty-six. That's not so much. After the eighth month, they're hardly considered premature anymore, right?"

"The baby's already over five pounds and very well developed," Bridget said, trying to buoy up her own courage. "If he's born now, he could probably hold his own. But I'm sure it's not that. I'm sure it's a false alarm.''

She held on to that thought for about thirty more seconds. Then she asked, ''Um, Nick? Do you really, really like this truck?''

He glanced over at her, as if he couldn't quite believe she wanted to discuss vehicles at a time like this. But he humored her. ''I like it okay, but I was thinking of trading it in for a four-door. Something more, you know, family oriented?''

She had to smile. He was trying so hard to please her, and succeeding admirably. ''Well, unfortunately, I think your trade-in value just went down.''

''Why's that?''

''My water broke.''

''Oh. Oh, my God. Then it really is happening.''

''Yup.'' Oddly, now that she knew the time was here, a sense of calm stole over her. It would be hours and hours before the baby actually made an appearance. They had plenty of time to get to the hospital. She reached into her purse and pulled out the index card of telephone numbers she'd compiled for this moment, including doctor, hospital, Liz, her mother, her insurance company. ''Can I use your car phone?''

Nick was already reaching for it. ''First, let me call Eric.''

''Eric? Why?''

''He's on the board of directors at the hospital. He'll make sure you get the best of care.''

''I would get the best of care, anyway,'' she protested. ''It's a good hospital.''

''Humor me. It'll only take a second.''

She let him call Eric, while she quietly endured

another labor pain. This one didn't seem as bad, more like a butcher knife instead of an ax plowing through her insides. Now that the end was in sight, she felt more optimistic and could endure the pain more easily.

"He'll be there in ten minutes," Nick said, handing her the phone. "Probably before we get there."

"He's actually coming to the hospital?"

"I told him if you didn't get the red carpet treatment, I'd beat him up."

"Hey, Nick. I have a great idea." She quickly dialed a number. "Liz? Bridget. Sorry to turn you right around, but I'm headed for the hospital...yes, doctors are stupid, and no, I'm not driving myself. My *fiancé* is driving me."

Nick could probably hear Liz's excited scream. "I'll be there in a flash," Liz said.

"I would think," Nick said after Bridget had disconnected, "that you would have more things to worry about than playing matchmaker."

"But they're perfect for each other."

Nick laughed. "I think it's more a case of that they deserve each other."

It was all Liz could do not to floor it as she made her tedious way down the icy back roads toward the hospital. How could Bridget be in labor when she still had almost a month to go? Surely she was mistaken. She'd just seen the doctor. Couldn't a doctor figure these things out? Or had he been in such a hurry to catch his plane that he hadn't been paying attention to Bridget's symptoms?

The backroads might have been a mistake, she

conceded as her car squiggled this way and that. At least the highway traffic would melt the ice. But she was worried about getting into a traffic jam. About once a year Oaksboro had one, and today might be the day.

She finally made it without mishap, though much later than she'd planned. She grabbed the first parking space she found in the visitor lot and ran for the hospital entrance, as much to escape the sharp wind as to get to her sister.

"Why today?" she despaired, heading unerringly for the maternity floor. Because they'd actually rehearsed for this moment, she knew exactly where to go.

A nurse directed her to Bridget's labor room, a homey little alcove of a room that looked like somebody's parlor—except for the hospital bed. Bridget wasn't in the bed, however. She was seated on a sofa—reclining in Nick's arms.

"Bridget, are you okay?" Liz went to her and hugged her gingerly. "Are you really having a baby? Shouldn't you be in bed? Are you and Nick really getting married?"

Bridget smiled wanly. "Yes, I'm having a baby, no, I'm more comfortable here for now, and yes, say hello to your future brother-in-law."

Liz squealed like a schoolgirl and threw her arms around Nick. "That's so cool! When? Can I be a bridesmaid?"

Someone tapped on the door.

"Come in!" Liz said exuberantly.

"Do you mind?" Bridget complained. "It's my labor room."

"Maybe it's the doctor," Nick said.

But the man who entered was definitely not a doctor. Liz backed up against the wall and tried to be invisible.

"Eric!" Nick jumped up, nearly depositing Bridget on the floor, and shook his brother's hand. "Thanks for coming. Bridget, all your problems are over. Eric will whip this place into shape and have every doctor and nurse—"

"I'm on the board of directors," Eric interrupted. "I'm not the chief of staff. I'm afraid I don't wield that much power around here." He shrugged apologetically, then looked straight at Liz. "Ah, if it isn't the mother of my child."

"Eric!" Liz objected.

"What's wrong? Don't you want everybody to know?" He held his arms up and shouted, "Liz Van Zandt is having my baby!"

"Eric!" she cried again. "What has gotten into you?"

He grinned at her. "The joy of impending fatherhood."

"He really is a changed man," Nick added helpfully, just as Bridget made a noise that sounded like a cat caught in a bicycle chain.

Everyone's concern went immediately to Bridget.

"Oh, my goodness," Eric said.

"Pant!" Liz commanded, grabbing Bridget's hand. "Squeeze my hand if you have to."

"What do you want us to do?" Nick asked.

After a few moments Bridget's contraction subsided. She pointed at Eric. "You go find me a doctor or a nurse. I am in premature labor and not even an orderly at this godforsaken crackerbox of a hospital has looked at me.''

''That's the problem I was going to mention,'' Eric said. ''Your obstetrician is on his way to Vale, and his associate had a car accident trying to get here.''

''Is she okay?'' Bridget asked, her brow furrowing with concern.

''She broke her arm. She won't be delivering any babies today.''

''How hard could it be to find another obstetrician?'' Nick fumed.

''We'll find one, don't worry.''

''Oh, I'm not worried,'' Bridget said. ''But you better find me a doctor or I'm going to make *you* deliver this kid!''

''Now, Bridget,'' Liz said in a soothing voice, not quite sure how to deal with this temper tantrum from her normally tranquil sister. ''Remember what they taught us in class. Childbirth makes us a little more cranky than usual, and we need to remember that our friends and relatives are likely to be as scared and stressed out as we are.''

''Oh, shut up.''

''Bridget!'' Liz said indignantly. ''Is that any way to talk?''

Bridget pointed at Nick. ''You sit back down. I need a back rest. And *you*…'' She pointed at Liz. ''Out. I don't care where you go, just leave.''

Eric grabbed Liz's arm. ''C'mon, Miss Manners, let's blow this joint.''

''But I'm her labor coach.''

''I think the lovebirds want to be alone.''

Chapter Fifteen

Liz let Eric lead her out of the room, but the moment they were alone in the corridor, she turned on him. "If you're not going to throw your weight around, you can go. We appreciate your efforts, but this is a family matter."

Eric headed resolutely down the corridor as if he knew where he was going. "In case you missed something, I *am* family. I'm related to you in ways that are going to become obvious soon enough, and I'm about to be related to your sister through marriage. That kid about to be born is the rough equivalent of my niece or nephew."

Liz had never thought of it that way. "Does that mean you'll be my brother-in-law?"

"Half brother-in-law. If you want to get technical." Eric stopped at the nurse's station. "Excuse me."

All conversation immediately stopped, and every female nurse within a fifty-foot radius froze and paid attention. And what red-blooded woman could stop herself from looking, Liz wanted to know. He was still the most handsome, charismatic man she'd ever seen.

"My sister-in-law is giving birth a month early, she's in considerable pain, and she needs medical attention. I appreciate how quickly you got her checked in, but an empty room and a hospital gown do not qualify as medical attention."

"We've got calls in to just about every obstetrician on our list," one nurse explained. "Dr. Cassidy broke her arm, Dr. Preece can't get his car out of his driveway—"

"You mean to tell me there's not a doctor in this hospital who can—"

"Dr. Bowman is in the delivery room right now doing an emergency cesarean. I'm not sure when he'll be free."

"Then how about an internist? A nurse practitioner? A podiatrist? I want someone with some degree of medical knowledge to examine Ms. Van Zandt in the next five minutes, or…or…"

"Or we'll sue the hospital!" Liz said triumphantly.

The nurse shook her head sadly. "Now, that would be bright. I'll go have a look at Ms. Van Zandt, but her doctor already told me it was false labor, so don't get your shorts in a knot."

"False labor!" Liz cried. "Your water doesn't break when you're in false labor!"

The nurse's demeanor immediately changed. "Her water broke? When?"

"Before she even got here!"

"Well, why didn't somebody tell me that?" She turned to the other nurses. "Janice, get Dr. Rashad or Dr. Williams up here stat." The nurse stepped out from behind the desk and strode purposefully toward Bridget's labor room.

Liz looked at Eric. "A podiatrist?"

"You're the one who threatened to sue."

"What was wrong with that?"

"I own half the hospital."

"Oh. Then it's your fault they're so poorly staffed."

"Believe me, if we could get more doctors on staff here, we would. They all want to be at the big teaching or research facilities. It's hard to get doctors to come to Oaksboro, Texas."

"I don't see why. It's a perfectly nice community. Couldn't you just offer them more money?"

Eric gave her a long-suffering look. "And pay them with what? Managed care and insurance companies have taken away any hope for a profit this hospital ever had."

Liz felt an unexpected pang of compassion for Eric. This hospital was only one of dozens of headaches he had to worry about. If his holdings didn't make a profit, his stockholders probably got real testy, not to mention his father.

"What you need is a good advertising campaign," she said.

"I need a lot of things, Queen Elizabeth. But talking about business right now isn't one of them."

Her perfectly good and helpful suggestion rejected, Liz resisted the urge to retort. Eric Statler was an ogre, pure and simple, and he didn't deserve her brilliant ideas. "What now?"

Eric was about to answer when Nick came striding down the hall.

"She kicked you out, too?"

Nick nodded. "There's a family waiting room right around this corner."

The waiting room wasn't nearly as cheerful as Bridget's labor room. No plants, for one thing, and the pictures on the wall were definitely of the starving-artist variety.

"You should get Bridget to paint some pictures for in here," Liz said.

"I doubt the hospital could afford Bridget."

"You could ask. She might donate a couple, if you gave her a little brass plaque. It would be good advertising."

"I don't think this is the time to ask her," Eric said, choosing a chair as far away from Liz as he could get.

With a harrumph, Liz picked up a magazine and started reading an article about nutrition for baby parrots.

During the next couple of hours, Bridget allowed only Nick to stay with her—and she frequently kicked him out. The obstetrician doing the cesarean had finished up and had examined Bridget, declaring that although the baby was early, everything appeared to be progressing smoothly.

Liz, upset at being shut out, sat with her face behind a magazine, refusing to talk with anybody. Not that anybody, meaning Eric, would talk to her. He was busy with his cell phone, running his company.

"And, Sandra, make a note," she heard him say in a slightly louder voice than normal. "I want this waiting room on the maternity ward redecorated. I'll pay for it out of my own pocket if I have to. But people waiting hours and hours shouldn't have to look at these horrible paintings.''

Liz smiled behind her magazine.

A commotion at the door to the waiting room caused Liz to peek out. Then she wanted to sink into the carpet and blend in with the stains already there.

"Mom, Dad!" Eric exclaimed. "What are you doing here?"

"My first grandchild is being born," Geraldine declared, "and no one is keeping me away. Not even the ice storm of the decade."

"Said she'd walk here if I didn't drive her," Two groused. "You wouldn't believe how bad it's getting. Tree branches breaking, telephone wires in the middle of the street, cars in ditches right and left."

"Grandchild?" Eric said.

Liz couldn't help putting in her two cents. "If the baby is your niece or nephew, that would make it your mother's grandchild. Let's be consistent about these things."

"Liz!" Geraldine actually sounded pleased to see her. "I guess I should have figured you would be here. I've been wanting to call you, but Eric forbade me."

Liz looked at Eric. "Why'd you do that?"

"Because I didn't want her interfering until we'd had a chance to work things out."

Two took his reading glasses off and squinted at Liz. "Oh, so this is the, um, young lady who's caused my son to go completely off the deep end."

"Two," Geraldine said, a warning note in her voice, "I'll not have you upsetting the mother of our first—I mean our second—"

"You all know?" Liz asked, feeling a little sick.

"Eric did everything but announce it over the loudspeaker at the Super Bowl," Geraldine said. "He's so excited about this baby, Liz."

Liz risked a look at Eric. He'd turned his back and was once again on his cell phone.

"No, really, he is," Geraldine assured her. "He wants to do the right thing by you—"

"Mother, please," Eric objected, proving he'd been listening all along, "I can handle this."

"Apparently not, or you would be speaking to each other. Maybe I shouldn't speak for Eric," she amended, "but I can speak for myself. I want to know this baby. I want to spoil it, just the way I'm going to spoil Nick's new baby."

"It's not Nick's baby," Two said in a bored voice. "She went to a fertility clinic."

Geraldine walked over to stand in front of her husband, hands on hips, fire blazing in her eyes. "You listen to me, Eric Statler, *Junior*. A baby's parentage has very little to do with biology and a lot to do with love. Nick loves Bridget and he loves that baby, and it doesn't matter to him that he wasn't there when the egg was fertilized. The child is his because he loves it as a father should. Though how he ever learned to love like that, I'll never know. He certainly didn't learn it from you!"

Two just stared at his wife as if he'd never seen her before.

She wasn't finished. "If you ever say one word— *one word*—to either of the children we're about to be blessed with in this family about their not being our *real* grandchildren, or that they weren't planned or that anybody wasn't insane with delight at the idea of their coming into the world—'' she paused and gave Eric an arch look ''—I will leave you so fast your fat head will spin!''

Liz was touched by Mrs. Statler's fierce concern for the children.

''Geraldine,'' Two began humbly, ''I understand what you're saying, but this is hardly the time or place—''

''You're right. I should have said it thirty years ago before we married. I might have saved my son from being treated like a second-class citizen in his own household.''

''But then I wouldn't be here,'' Eric pointed out.

Geraldine turned on him. ''Oh, you be quiet. You're almost as bad as your father. Liz and I are going down to the cafeteria to have some tea, aren't we, dear?''

Liz gulped. ''Uh-huh.''

ERIC WATCHED HIS MOTHER all but drag Liz out of the waiting room. Maybe it wasn't such a bad thing. Maybe Geraldine could convince Liz to be a part of their family.

Ah, who was he kidding? At the moment, the Statler family appeared pretty dysfunctional. Liz might decide to up and move to Peru.

Eric looked over at his father, who appeared shell-shocked. ''Was I really that terrible to Nick?'' Two asked.

''You did play favorites sometimes,'' Eric said. ''Like, you never came to Nick's football games, but you always came to mine.''

"Nick said he didn't want me to come."

"Really?"

"Your mother always assumed I was the one who rejected Nick, but you have no idea how difficult a five-year-old boy can be, especially when he's battling you for his mother's affection."

"You mean Nick went Oedipal on us?"

"I tried to make friends with him. I really did. I took him to the State Fair one year, and I spent about a hundred bucks on one of those stupid games trying to win him a big tiger. And finally I did. And you know what he did?"

Eric couldn't imagine. He certainly hadn't heard this story from his brother.

"He gave it to a little raggedy kid as we were walking back to the car. And he wasn't just being generous. He did it to hurt me, to remind me I wasn't his real father. Oh, no, his *real* father was coming back some day to take him to a castle in England, just like Prince Valiant's."

"Nick?" Eric had never, ever heard Nick mention anything about his real father.

"Granted, he was just a little boy, but he resented the hell out of me. After a while I quit trying to mend fences with him. I just let him go his own way. Maybe I should have tried again, when he was old enough to understand, but by then we'd established a pattern of hostile tolerance, and I was afraid to rock the boat. If I'd driven him away, your mother never would have forgiven me."

Eric suspected his father was sugarcoating his role just a tad. He remembered times when Two had been downright hateful to Nick. Just bringing up the fact that Bridget had been artificially inseminated showed his attitude wasn't all sweetness and light. But maybe it would be a good idea if Eric and his mother remembered that every story has two sides.

"Just the same," Eric said, "you might try showing a little enthusiasm for Bridget's baby. If you accepted him or her into the family, it might go a long way toward healing whatever's wrong between you and Nick."

"Nick wouldn't know what to do if I suddenly went soft on him," Two said, putting his reading glasses back on and hiding behind his newspaper.

Eric sighed. Was Liz doomed to receive the same "hostile tolerance" as Nick had, just because she'd had the audacity to conceive a Statler baby out of wedlock? And because she wasn't the wife Two would have chosen for Eric?

Eric was relieved when they were joined in the waiting room by Bridget and Liz's mother, who greeted him with a wary smile. Then Nick returned, after Bridget kicked him out again. Finally Geraldine and Liz came back.

"How's the weather out there?" Eric asked Sophie, the twins' mother.

"Terrible. I thought I never would make it here. The temperature's dropped to eighteen degrees, and the wind blowing that ice—feels like needles."

"Yeah, Nick," Two said, never looking up from his newspaper. "Your kid picked a terrible time to make an appearance."

Nick appeared surprised, but he said nothing.

Eric smiled. Maybe his old man was coming around. But a glance at Liz and her steely expression caused his smile to fade. She wasn't softening in the least. Had he simply hurt her too badly with his hasty, ill-thought-out words, to ever make amends? Had he abused her trust in him so thoroughly that he could never win it back?

He'd made some changes in the past few weeks—not just in his thinking, but in his life. Maybe now was the time to tell her. He put down his magazine, hitched up his courage and stood up.

She gave him a warning look. He could almost read her mind: *Go away, I'm not up to this, not in front of all these people, not when my sister is in the middle of a birthing crisis and she won't even let me near her.*

Still, he wasn't going away. Whether she liked it or not, he was in this for the long haul. He purposefully made his way across the room and sat next to her. "You've been reading that same magazine for two hours."

"It's very interesting."

"*Bird Fancy?* Do you have any birds?"

"No, but maybe I'll get one."

"Are birds healthy to have around small children?" he asked.

"I don't know."

"You've been reading about birds for two hours and you don't know?"

"The question didn't come up! But if birds are in any way detrimental to a child's health, I won't get one, okay? You don't have much faith in my parenting abilities."

"Do you blame me? You don't want to give the kid a father."

"Not a part-time one."

This wasn't going as he'd planned. He hadn't meant to come over here and harass her. There was just something about her that brought out a competitive edge, and apparently he had the same effect on her. It seemed to him they could channel that competitiveness to good ends.

Then why don't you tell her that?

Eric jumped. He wasn't used to hearing little voices in his head. But the words had been unmistakable. Why didn't he tell Liz how he really felt about her?

Because you're afraid she won't return your feelings.

He was accustomed to taking all sorts of calculated risks in business, but when it came to love, he was afraid to commit himself without the reassurance of a sure thing. What a sobering realization.

"Liz..."

"Eric..." she said at the same time.

Then the lights went off, throwing the waiting room into total darkness.

Everyone started talking at once. Eric picked out his mother's startled voice, his father's gruff outrage, Nick's commonsense reassurances.

And Liz's soft cry of fear. The dark. She was afraid of the dark. Protective instincts roaring to life, he reached for her hand. "It's all right, darling," he said, the endearment slipping out. "There's nothing to be afraid of."

"How can they deliver Bridget's baby in the dark?" Liz whispered urgently.

A voice came over a speaker in the waiting room.

"Can I have your attention, please? Ladies and gentlemen, we've had a power outage due to the storm."

"No kidding," Two grumbled.

"The hospital's back-up generators ensure a seamless power supply to all surgical suites, treatment rooms and patient rooms, so you needn't worry for the safety of the patients."

"Oh, thank heavens," Sophie said.

"But it may be a few minutes before we restore power to visitor areas such as waiting rooms, rest rooms and the cafeteria. If you are in the dark, please just sit still. The staff is distributing flashlights and battery-powered lanterns."

"There, now, you see?" Eric said, speaking softly into Liz's ear. The scent of her hair was driving him wild. "There's nothing to worry about. Bridget's being taken care of."

"I don't like the dark."

"I know. But you're safe. I won't let anything hurt you."

Her grip on his hand loosened slightly. "You know what's funny?"

"What?"

"I believe you."

"I love you, Liz. Even when I was angry with you, and even when I was acting like a jerk, I still loved you. I would never want to see you hurt. And I hate it that I've made you sad and worried."

"Oh, Eric, I love you, too, even though I haven't exactly been Miss Congeniality. When I said I wanted you to sign those awful papers for the child's sake, I can't deny I was being vengeful, too."

He stroked her cheek, surprised to find it damp.

"Maybe we're both a little too used to getting our own way."

"And maybe we both need to work on controlling our tempers."

"Learning to compromise."

"Learning to listen to each other," she said.

"We're doing that now."

"Hey, we are. We always do better when the lights are off, have you noticed that?"

Eric realized she was right. In the dark their relationship was broken down into its most basic components. In the dark it was easier to remember the laughter, the tenderness, the love they shared as anonymous paramours in a shadowy pantry, and as co-conspirators to passion in a luxurious, but dark, hotel suite. "Liz. Can we hold on to these feelings with the lights on?"

"I want to, Eric. I really do."

"In that case—" he took a deep breath "—when's the wedding?"

He'd never found Liz to be at a loss for words, but here was a new first.

"Hey, you're the one who proposed," he said. "I'm accepting." When she still didn't say anything, he added, "You mean you weren't serious when you asked me to marry you at the Shop'N'Save?"

"You must never, ever tell our child I proposed to you at a grocery store."

"It'll be one of my favorite bedtime stories. So…?"

"How would you feel about a double wedding with Bridget and Nick? You see, Bridget and I always fantasized about getting married on the same day with matching white gowns...well, maybe off-white under the circumstances.''

Eric relaxed and slid his arm around Liz's shoulders. ''Whatever you want, just so it's soon.'' Even in the total darkness, Eric had no trouble finding Liz's mouth. It was the softest thing in the vicinity. He kissed her with all his love and passion and commitment, and even though he wasn't sure you could say all those things in just a kiss, he could have sworn she returned the same emotions.

Eric didn't know the lights were back on until he realized the rest of the waiting room was applauding. Slowly he and Liz separated. Her face turned bright-pink, and he wasn't sure that his own didn't do the same.

''Shoot, if I'd known it was this easy to get you two together,'' Nick said, ''I'd have thrown you in the storm cellar long ago.''

Eric was saved from a suitably smart reply when a nurse with an armload of flashlights entered the waiting room. ''Guess we won't be needing these. Is everybody here okay?''

''Hunky-dory,'' Two said. It didn't escape Eric's attention that his parents were holding hands. He and Liz weren't the only ones to find understanding in the dark.

''Which one of you is Ms. Van Zandt's labor coach?''

''That would be me,'' Liz said, popping out of her chair.

''She's asking for you. We're moving her to the delivery room now.''

Liz darted for the door, the newly acknowledged

love of her life forgotten for the moment. That was
okay, though, Eric thought, smiling to himself. He
felt confident she would remember him soon enough,
and then he would get all of her attention—for the
rest of their lives.

Epilogue

Oaksboro was making up for a miserably cold winter with a stifling summer. The Statler family was gathered in the library—everyone but Two.

Nick bided his time watching Bridget. He never tired of watching his wife, even if she was only straightening their daughter's bonnet. Charlotte, now five and a half months old, was busy wiggling around on the antique Chinese rug, gurgling delightedly as she tested its softness with her nose.

Liz, looking regal but wilted in her designer maternity dress, sat next to Eric on the leather sofa—the same sofa where Nick had made love to Bridget for the first time. None of them appreciated the heat, but Liz in particular was tired of it.

"Did someone turn off the air-conditioning?" she asked.

"It's up as high as it will go," Eric answered, pushing a damp strand of hair off her forehead. "Let me get you a glass of lemonade. Or that decaffeinated raspberry iced tea you like."

"No, that's all right. I'll float away if I drink anything else. Where is Two, anyway? Isn't he the one who called this mysterious meeting?''

''Yeah, and I wish he'd hurry up and get here,'' Nick said. ''The Rangers game starts in ten minutes.''

Bridget gave him a reproving look. ''Lighten up, will you? He must have a pretty good reason for calling us together.''

Nick started to make a smart reply, then thought better of it. Gradually his lovely wife was breaking him of a lot of bad habits where Two was concerned. Nick had been so accustomed to needling his stepfather over any little thing that he didn't even realize he was doing it. But Bridget—and his mother and Eric and Liz, too—all had been deftly reminding him that it took two people to form a bad relationship, and he was one of them.

He'd sensed a subtle difference in Two, too. Every once in a while the old man would make a small gesture—giving Nick the biggest steak, or complimenting his new car. He'd been especially nice to Bridget, going out of his way to make her feel welcome in their home, and for that alone, Nick had been trying to do better where Two was concerned.

Two entered the library a short time later. Geraldine met him at the door and slipped her arm through his. Nick's mother was beaming like a lighthouse, and Nick knew then that whatever announcement Two was planning to make, it wasn't bad news.

Two carried a sheaf of papers, and he handed out packets to Nick, Eric and each of their wives.

''The family dynamics have changed a bit in the past few months,'' Two said, ''and I realized my old will was no good anymore. So I've drawn up a new one. You don't have to read the whole thing, of course, but I've highlighted a few pertinent passages.''

Nick flipped through the pages apprehensively until his own name caught his eye.

''For my son, Nicholas Allen Raines, who shall for the purposes of this document be viewed as my true and legal heir…'' Nick's eyes blurred. But that was okay. He didn't have to read the specific bequests. The words *my son, Nicholas* were enough.

Bridget was surprised to find herself mentioned specifically by name. ''To my son Nicholas's wife, Bridget Van Zandt Raines…'' He'd left her a huge stock portfolio, because he felt every woman should have ''a little something'' in her own name. ''And for Charlotte Aileen Raines, my granddaughter…'' A trust fund that, when mature in eighteen years, would provide more than enough for tuition to any university she chose. Bridget dabbed at her eyes. That sly old devil.

Eric was not surprised, but neither was he disappointed, to see that his previous inheritance had dwindled considerably. Not that he would be left high and dry. He would still own a large share of Statler Enterprises, worth millions—so long as he kept the company profitable. That end was virtually guaranteed, since he had, with his father's approval, delegated responsibility for various divisions to his father's most trusted managers. Eric had drastically changed his own job description so that now he focused on what he did best—troubleshooting, working with the rank and file employees to see that the troops stayed happy. Redecorating an occasional waiting room. And coming home at five every night.

Liz couldn't believe her father-in-law's generosity. As his son, Eric would someday inherit a sizable chunk of change, and Liz and all of their children would of course benefit, too. But he'd gone to the trouble to mention Liz by name and had selected a bequest that would mean something to her. He was giving her her own ad agency, and it happened to be the one she worked for.

"Wait till my boss hears that someday I'll be writing *his* paychecks. If I don't fire the jerk first. Not for a very long time, I hope," she added, lest Two think she was looking forward to his demise.

But that wasn't all. Two had provided a generous scholarship fund for her soon-to-be-born offspring.

"Um, Two," she said as diplomatically as possible, "are there provisions for, oh, let's say, future children?"

Bridget gave her a horrified look. "Liz! Let's not be greedy."

"It's just that, well, I want things to be equitable between the, um, twins."

"Twins!" The word reverberated around the room.

"Liz!" Bridget hopped up from her chair, looking annoyingly slim. "You're having twins? You told me you didn't even know the child's sex!"

"We wanted to keep the twins a surprise," Eric said sheepishly. "And we don't know their sexes. Really."

"You might have gotten a head start on me in the children department," Liz said triumphantly, pointing her finger at Bridget, "but I'm about to pull ahead!"

Nick and Eric looked at each other with sort of "uh-oh" expressions. "They're competing?" Nick asked.

"We compete in everything," Liz said cheerfully. "Or haven't you noticed—oh!"

"What?" everyone asked at once.

"Nothing, just a—ouch!"

"I'm sure it's nothing to worry about," Eric said, sounding more as if he wanted to reassure himself than anyone else. "She still has almost a month to go."

Bridget got a strange look on her face. "Liz, how many days till your due date?"

"Twenty-six," Liz managed to answer, which was no easy task when her body felt like it was trying to turn itself inside out.

"Call the hospital. And the doctor," Bridget said. "There's no need to panic, she's got plenty of time, but ten-to-one this is the real thing."

And with the efficiency of a general, Bridget collected Charlotte, herded everyone to their various tasks and got them all to the hospital in record time.

Liz had sworn she wouldn't disgrace herself the way her sister had by bellowing and cursing and kicking everybody out of her labor room, but she did, anyway, until the very last moment when she let Eric and Bridget witness the delivery.

At exactly the hour predicted, she gave birth to small but healthy identical twin boys.

"They are beautiful," Eric said. He praised Liz's

efforts, claiming no woman in the world had ever given birth with such natural talent and flair.

"They're handsome," Liz corrected him.

"Have you thought of names?" Bridget asked.

"We could name them both Eric," Eric joked. "How would you like to call our sons Four and Five?"

Our sons. Liz closed her eyes and savored those words. She grabbed on to Bridget's hand. "Well, Sis, mission accomplished."

Bridget beamed back a smile that lit up the delivery room.

* * * * *

In April 2001, look for Kara Lennox's exciting contribution to the captivating
2001 WAYS TO WED *series,*
only from Harlequin American Romance!

TEXAS CONFIDENTIAL

Penny Archer has always been the
dependable and hardworking executive
assistant for Texas Confidential, a secret
agency of Texas lawmen. But her daring
heart yearned to be the heroine of her
own adventure—and to find a love
that would last a lifetime.

And this time...

THE SECRETARY GETS HER MAN
by Mindy Neff

Coming in January 2001 from

 HARLEQUIN®

AMERICAN *Romance*

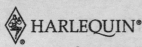

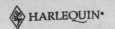

Tyler Brides

It happened one weekend...

Quinn and Molly Spencer are delighted to accept three bookings for their newly opened B&B, Breakfast Inn Bed, located in America's favorite hometown, Tyler, Wisconsin.

But Gina Santori is anything but thrilled to discover her best friend has tricked her into sharing a room with the man who broke her heart eight years ago....

And Delia Mayhew can hardly believe that she's gotten herself locked in the Breakfast Inn Bed basement with the sexiest man in America.

Then there's Rebecca Salter. She's turned up at the Inn in her wedding gown. Minus her groom.

Come home to Tyler for three delightful novellas by three of your favorite authors: Kristine Rolofson, Heather MacAllister and Jacqueline Diamond.

HARLEQUIN®
Makes any time special ™

PHTB